ur excitement, all our passion, all our high
s had just drained away in seconds, like
one had pulled out a plug. I bit my lip. I felt
I'd been on top of the world, soaring through
clouds, and someone had pulled me cruelly back
'n to earth with a bump...

F

For Madison

www.thebeautifulgamebooks.co.uk

ORCHARD BOOKS
338 Euston Road, London NW1 3BH
Orchard Books Australia
Level 17/207 Kent Street, Sydney, NSW 2000

First published in 2010 by Orchard Books

ISBN 978 1 40830 423 5

Text © Narinder Dhami 2010

1 3 5 7 9 10 8 6 4 2
Printed in Great Britain

Orchard Books is a division of Hachette Children's Books,
an Hachette UK company.

www.hachette.co.uk

THE BEAUTIFUL GAME

Friends and football – the perfect match

GEORGIE'S WAR

NARINDER DHAMI

ORCHARD BOOKS

PROLOGUE

Friday 10.30pm

I AM SO ANGRY RIGHT NOW, I COULD JUST THROW MY DIARY STRAIGHT OUT OF THE WINDOW!

I know that Grace, Hannah and the other girls think I have a really bad temper. I try to bite my lip and count to ten and breathe through my nose and calm down, but when something gets to me, I just can't seem to hold back.

Mum always used to say that there was a little angel Georgie sitting on one of my shoulders, and a naughty devil Georgie on the other, whispering in my ears, telling me what to do. And, OK, I admit it, sometimes naughty Georgie wins. Sometimes? Well, quite often!

I'm not just angry now, though, I'm upset. I don't think I'm going over the top, either. Anyone would be upset if they'd seen what I saw tonight.

Today started like any other normal day. I went to school. I did my homework when I got back, and then I went to the park to meet Hannah, Jasmin and the others, like I always do the night before a Stars match. And then it happened.

How can everything be fine one minute, and then suddenly it all goes wrong?

Why do things always have to change?

CHAPTER ONE

'Luke! Get *off* me!' I roared, kicking my arms and legs furiously. I was being pinned down on the sofa by my idiot brother, and he was piling cushions on top of me.

'Give in, then, and tell me where it is!' Luke yelled. He chucked another cushion on top of the heap, and then leaned heavily on them so that I couldn't get up. His face was bright red and his long black hair was sticking up and out all over the place. Luke always thinks he's *so* cool with his millions of girlfriends – wouldn't it be funny if one of them could see him right now?

'NO!' Gritting my teeth, I managed to fight my way up through the barrier of cushions. I gave Luke a shove he wasn't expecting, and he went staggering backwards across the living room. 'You're not having it!'

'OW!' Luke hit his toe on the coffee table and gave a loud, dramatic groan. Honestly, what *is* it with men and pain? They always have to make a big deal of it – and I should know, living with three brothers and a dad. If they get a sniffle, it's, like, a major health crisis. No wonder it's women that have babies. Men would *never* be able to cope with *that*!

I giggled at the look on Luke's face, and he glared at me.

'I'm telling Dad!' he burst out.

'We interrupt this argument to bring you an important piece of breaking news,' I said in my best, annoying, American accent. '*Luke Tells Dad!*'

Luke's eyes narrowed. 'Right, give me that remote control RIGHT NOW, Georgie, or you're deader than the deadest thing in the entire universe!' he shouted.

'Tough!' I retorted. '*I* was here first, and *I* want to watch *The Vampire Chronicles*!'

I settled myself down on the sofa again next to Rainbow, our black cat. Rainbow hadn't moved an inch while Luke was trying to smother me with cushions. In fact, he hadn't even opened his eyes. Rainbow was pretty old now – my mum had found him starving in the street fifteen years ago, when my brother Jack was still a baby, and had brought him home. Rainbow was a bit deaf now, which probably wasn't a bad thing, living in this house.

Luke frowned. Then he spun round and switched the TV off, turning back to grin annoyingly at me.

'Put that TV on!' I howled.

Luke folded his arms. 'Make me.'

Fuming, I flew across the room just as the door opened. Dad walked in, and I crashed straight into him.

'OOF!' Dad gasped, as I knocked the breath out of him. 'What's going on in here? It sounds like World War Three yet again.'

Luke and I both began yelling at the same time.

'*I* want to watch *The Vampire Chronicles*!' I shrieked.

'Well, *I* want to watch a documentary about space travel!' Luke roared. 'It's for school,' he added, glancing virtuously at Dad.

'Oh, please!' I snapped. 'You mean you want to see *Sun and Fun in Ibiza*, so that you can drool over girls in bikinis—'

'STOP!' Dad yelled, sticking his fingers in his ears. 'This is why you both have TVs in your bedrooms.'

'But I want to watch the big flatscreen in here,' Luke and I whined at exactly the same moment. I don't know why we argue so much. Maybe it's because Luke is only two years older than I am. But I honestly don't remember us fighting this much before Mum died...

'What will it take for you two to get along a bit better?' Dad went on, raising his eyes to heaven. 'I wish I knew!' Poor old Dad, he seems to be getting more and more fed up every day with all the rows. 'Luke, go and do your homework. Georgie, go and get ready for football training. Adey's going to drop you off at the college.' He held up his hand as Luke and I both opened our mouths again. 'No, I *really* don't want to hear it. I've had a hard day at the office. Now get out of here, the pair of you.'

Luke stalked off, looking deeply annoyed. I scooted after him, secretly wondering if I could trip him up in the hall and then get to the safety of my bedroom before he caught me. On the other hand,

I decided maybe I'd let him off this time. I was *much* more excited about getting ready for the first training session of the new season. I couldn't *wait* to see the other girls. Well, I'd seen Hannah, Grace and Katy at school today, and all six of us had got together at least once every week since the season finished. Lauren had had her birthday in May, and her parents, who are *seriously* loaded, booked a day at a Brazilian soccer school for the six of us. It was a great laugh. You wouldn't *believe* the tricks we can do with a football now!

We'd also met up with Freya Reynolds, our fantabulous coach, a few times too. Mr and Mrs Fleetwood, Hannah's parents, had had a barbeque in their back garden during the summer holidays, and they'd invited Freya as well as us girls and our parents. It had been big fun, even though Olivia, Hannah's snooty half-sister, had ignored us!

But nothing could beat the excitement of us all getting together at our VERY FIRST training session of the season. That was beyond special. The Springhill Stars Under-Thirteens team was back in business. YAY! And I just *knew* we were going to get promotion to the top league this season, I could feel it in my bones.

'Georgie?'

I turned around as I reached the door.

'Yes, Dad?'

'Where's the remote control?' asked Dad, the ghost of a twinkle in his eye.

I went over to the sofa and stuck my hand between Rainbow and the cushion. Rainbow gave a sleepy chirrup as I pulled out the remote control from underneath his fluffy tail.

'Thank you,' Dad said.

I left him watching the news and went upstairs. Luke had vanished into his room, sulking probably, but Jack was coming down as I went up.

'What's happening, Fishface?' he said, giving me a punch on the shoulder.

'Ow,' I said automatically, even though it didn't really hurt. 'Don't do that, Ugly Mug.'

Jack tried to punch me again, but this time I slapped his hand away. We wrestled for a bit, trying to push each other down the stairs (don't panic, we were only a few steps up). Then Dad came out of the living room and told us to be quiet, he couldn't hear the news.

Jack and I get on slightly better than Luke and me, but not *that* much, to be honest with you. Jack's sixteen, two years older than Luke, but they're good mates, so Jack usually takes his side. They both tease me and try to boss me around, but I don't put up with any of their garbage. I stand up for myself and speak out. I have to, otherwise my voice would just get lost in the all-male crowd in this house.

I shoved my way past Jack, ran upstairs and burst into my bedroom, humming the theme tune from *Match of the Day*. There I threw off my school uniform and dragged my Spurs shirt and a pair of navy trackie bottoms out of my wardrobe. It was early September but the weather was still quite warm, so I grabbed an old denim jacket that used to belong to Dad, and slung it on over the top. That would do fine. Then I scraped back my masses of black, curly hair and held it off my face with a black stretchy headband that had *definitely* seen better days.

So I expect you've guessed by now that you're unlikely to see me in the front row of the audience at London Fashion Week! Honestly, I just can't be *bothered* with all that girlie stuff. Grace asked me once if I'd always been a tomboy, or if I act this way because I want to be like my brothers. I didn't know what to say. I *thought* I'd always been like this, but

I remember loving to watch my mum putting on her make-up and helping her choose what to wear, when I was a little girl...

But anyway, I'd never hear the end of it from Luke and Jack if I went all glam and girlie now. They'd laugh their heads off. I couldn't be doing with that.

I took my purple Springhill Stars shirt and put it carefully in my sports bag, along with my white shorts. Freya doesn't mind if we don't wear our match kits for training, but it's become a tradition that we all wear them at the very first session of the new season. It kind of *reminds* us how important the team is, and gets us off to a great start.

Thinking of Freya, I remembered I had something to ask her. I took my battered old mobile out of my pocket and rattled off a text message.

Hi, Freya, can I talk to u after training 2nite?

A reply came whizzing back about two seconds later.

Sure! C u soon, F.

Smiling, I slipped my phone back into my pocket. I'd been playing for the Stars ever since I was eight years old. Freya was my coach for that first season, then, as I'd got older and moved into different teams – Under-Tens, Under-Elevens, and so on – I'd had other coaches. But Freya was the one I liked the most, so I was dead pleased when she took over the Under-Thirteens. She'd been really kind to me when my mum died.

Freya was straight down the line. You always knew where you stood with her. And she's so cool. She rides a motorbike, a huge big shiny thing! I think she's great, even though we've had some fierce run-ins over the years.

What do you mean, Georgie? I hear you say. *Surely you're a pussycat on the pitch?*

Ha ha – get real! Although I'm in goal and I'm not even the captain of the team, I yell and shout at the others all the time. I rant and rave and I get *furious*. I don't mean anything horrible by it, I just can't help it. I get so caught up in the match, I *have* to let some of that intensity out, or I'd burst! I know I go a bit too far sometimes, though. It's something I have to watch. Now that Jasmin, Lauren, Grace, Hannah, Katy and me are so solid, I don't want to do anything to mess that up. Been there, nearly done that, just a few months ago when I had that big bust-up with Lauren...

I clattered downstairs, bag in hand, and jumped down the last few steps. Dad was still in the living room, and was now on the phone to his sister, our

Aunt Celie, in Jamaica. Luke had abandoned his homework and sneaked downstairs again, and he and Jack were sprawled on the sofa, annoying each other the way boys do. You know, one kicks the other, and then they start grabbing each other's arms and trying to twist them, and just generally acting like little kids. Luke and Jack are *so* good at that.

'Ready, Georgie?' Adey came in, tall and lanky, wearing his Melfield United jacket, his shoulder-length dark hair tied back.

'Yep.' I grinned at him. Thank God I get on with *one* of my brothers. But then, Adey's nearly eighteen, and he's a lot more mature than Batman and Robin over there. He's a good football player, too – an attacking midfielder – and he's an apprentice at our town's league club, Melfield United. Adey's hoping he'll get a professional contract there when his two-year apprenticeship finishes.

'Oh, I forgot.' Luke jumped to his feet and began prancing around the living room, flicking back his hair. 'It's the Purple Petunias' girlie get-together tonight, isn't it?'

I tried not to react. Luke and Jack love football as much as I do, and they both play for the school team. But that doesn't stop them from teasing me the whole time, and they have this ridiculous name for the Stars, which totally winds me up.

'If you mean it's the Springhill Stars' training session tonight, then yes,' I replied as calmly as I could. Meaning, not really very calmly at all!

'A training session isn't having a chat about clothes and make-up and stuff,' Jack scoffed.

Adey was shaking his head. 'You daft pair still living in the Dark Ages, then?' he said with a grin. 'Have you *seen* the standard of women's football in this country recently?'

'When sixty thousand people want to go and watch Georgie and her little mates, instead of Manchester United, I might change my mind,' Jack chortled.

Luke aimed a weak little kick at an imaginary ball. 'Oh no,' he squealed in a high-pitched voice, 'I've smudged my pedicure!'

'You're such an *idiot*, Luke,' I snapped. 'I don't know how Lucy puts up with you.' Lucy was Luke's current air-head blonde girlfriend. I hadn't met her so far, but all his other girlfriends have been blonde air-heads, so I can't imagine Lucy's any different. 'Oh, yes, I forgot. She's going out with you, so she must be daft as you are.'

'Give it a rest, you two,' Dad said absent-mindedly.

He must have heard this kind of conversation a million times before, so I didn't blame him for not taking much notice. Anyway, Dad's pretty quiet and it takes a lot to make him lose his rag. It was Mum who always used to wade in and break up our fights. She could shout louder than any of us!

Luke had now begun heading his imaginary ball. 'I've ruined my new hairdo!' he shrieked, pretending to break down in tears.

Adey took one look at my face and dragged me out of the house.

'Rise above it, Gorgeous George,' he told me as we climbed into his ancient Volkswagen.

'But they never stop,' I complained bitterly. 'Not ever. I wouldn't care, but they haven't been to watch *any* of my matches for the last three years—'

'I've told you this a million times, Georgie.' Adey swung the car in the direction of Melfield College where the Stars played their matches and had their training sessions. 'It's not really about you. Luke and Jack wind each other up, too, all the time. Jack has a go about Luke's girlfriends changing from one minute to the next, and Luke has a dig about Jack's punky mates. And they're always having a pop at me, too. It's just the way they are.'

I was silent. In a way, I knew that Adey was right. But secretly, I was a bit hurt by some of the things that Luke and Jack said to me. I tried not to care, but I did. I would have *died* rather than show it, though. I knew that if I revealed just once, even slightly, that maybe I wasn't *quite* as tough and tomboyish as Jack and Luke, as everyone else seemed to think I was, that I'd just get teased even more. It was sink or swim in our house...

God, I don't know why I'm going on like this – it must be because you're such a good listener. Just ignore me. I can cope, honestly!

As we turned into the college car park, Grace, Hannah and Katy were waiting on the steps, and Lauren was jumping out of her mum's silver sports car. My face split into a huge grin. As Adey drew to a halt, Mrs Sharma's little red banger pulled up behind us, and I looked round and saw Jasmin hanging out of the window, waving at me.

'Don't forget to ask Freya about the Open Day,' Adey reminded me as I opened the car door.

'I'm seeing her after training.' I bounded out of the car, excitement fizzing through my insides. 'Thanks, Adey. See you later.'

I turned round and was swamped by a human

whirlwind. Jasmin, Lauren, Katy, Grace and Hannah all fell on me and pulled me into a circle of arms.

'The Springhill Stars are back!' Jasmin squealed, dangerously close to my left ear. 'Big group hug!'

We all jumped up and down in a tangle as we squeezed the breath out of each other. I'm not *really* a huggy, touchy-feely person, but secretly I don't mind that much!

'Who's up for promotion this year then?' Lauren demanded.

'WE ARE!' everyone yelled.

'And who's up for the County Cup?' Lauren went on.

'WE ARE!' we screamed. We were getting a few funny looks from people arriving at the college for their evening classes, but did we care? NO, WE DIDN'T!

'Cool.' Lauren slapped me on the back. 'Better stop letting in so many goals, then, Georgie.'

'Cheeky monkey!' I slapped *her* on the back, but not very hard because Lauren's tiny, about half my size. 'How about you, Grace, Hannah and Jasmin start knocking in a few more down the other end?'

'Ooh, that's *so* unfair,' Jasmin pouted, flicking back her gorgeous silky black hair. 'I'm more of a *defensive* midfielder.'

'Meaning, you've got two left feet in front of goal?' Hannah suggested gently.

'I've got two left feet *everywhere*,' sighed Jasmin, and we all shrieked with laughter. It's true, she's just a *teensy* bit clumsy.

'Anyway, Grace was the third top goal-scorer in our league, even though we missed out on promotion,' Katy pointed out.

'That's very true,' Grace agreed, her blue eyes dancing. 'Which obviously means I need to find a team more worthy of my fantastic skills.'

We all jeered loudly, in a friendly way though, as we went through the college doors. Grace is *so* not swollen-headed at all, and she's got every right to be because she's tall and blonde and beautiful and a lovely person, as well as a fantastic footballer.

I glanced sideways at my *brilliant* mates as we skidded down the corridors, heading towards the sports facilities at the back of the college, all of us talking at once. I'd known Grace the longest because she'd started playing for the Stars around the same time as me, and then Lauren and Jasmin had joined the team a year or two later. The four of us had liked each other and we'd got on OK, but we hadn't become *really* friendly until Katy and Hannah joined the Stars earlier this year, and Freya sent the six of us on a week-long intensive training course. We'd bonded like superglue! But we'd had a few dodgy moments and bitter fallings-out along the way...

I sneaked a peek at Lauren, who was bouncing along beside me, shiny blonde hair swinging. She and Grace were the glam ones, always wearing make-up and the latest clothes. Lauren had a fearsome temper like me, though, and I still squirmed uncomfortably when I remembered how we'd clashed just before the end of last season. We'd both been so stubborn, it had nearly split the group apart until the other girls took over and forced us to make up. The row had been mostly Lauren's fault to start with, but I'd made it much worse with my attitude. I'd kind of thought that Lauren had it all – nice mum and dad, big house, flash cars, lots of money – and I'd been a bit jealous. Then, when we'd found out that Lauren was very unhappy, I'd felt *terrible*. I was going to make it up to her, though.

'Talking about me having two left feet,' Jasmin began. She slipped slightly on the polished floor as she spoke, which of course sent the rest of us in hysterical laughter. 'I'll just remind you that I was the best at those heel flicks we learned at the Brazilian soccer skills day.'

'Oh, that was so cool, wasn't it?' Lauren laughed. 'The most fantastic birthday I ever had.'

'You *were* great at those heels flicks, Jas,' Katy agreed. 'But what about that trick where we had to flip the ball over the top of our partners? You nearly knocked my head off!'

'That's one way of stopping your opponent, I suppose,' Hannah said thoughtfully, 'beheading them with the football.'

Jasmin collapsed into giggles. And when Jasmin giggles, the rest of us follow! She's a bit dippy, but she's got lots of personality, and a bit of a wacky dress sense. Today she was wearing a pink beanie hat with a big, floppy purple flower stuck on the side and a clashing lime-green jacket with a funky red velvet trim.

Hannah seemed very quiet when she joined the Stars, but she's really fun and some of the things she says have us in fits of laughter. Katy's the mystery girl out of all of us. I don't mean that in a nasty way, it's just that we don't know much about her family, really.

They never come to the matches, and Katy sometimes can't go out with us because she has to look after her little brother. She's quite serious-looking with big, solemn brown eyes, but when she smiles, you can see the *real* Katy.

The six of us hurtled down the corridor to the changing-room. As we got closer we could hear the sound of chanting coming from inside.

'FIVE-FOUR-THREE-TWO!'

As we reached the open door, Ruby, Jo-Jo, Debs, Emily and Alicia, the rest of our team, were waiting for us.

'ONE!' they yelled, leaping on us. 'WE HAVE LIFT-OFF! GO, SPRINGHILL STARS!'

We had another team hug, chattering at the tops of our voices. As you can probably tell by now, we were all incredibly overexcited!

'Oh, we're late!' Grace exclaimed, glancing around the changing-room. The other Stars teams had already gone outside. 'We'd better get changed.'

'Freya must be late too, then,' Hannah pointed out, pulling off her white jacket. 'Because she's usually in here like a shot if we're not ready on time.'

We got changed as fast as possible and then headed out of the changing-room in one big, happy gang.

'Are you bringing Chelsea to the match on Saturday, Lauren?' asked Jasmin as we made our way to the football pitches. The other Stars teams and their coaches were already well stuck into their training – we *were* pretty late. 'After all, she's our official mascot now.'

Lauren nodded. 'You'll be amazed at how well-behaved Chelsea is,' she told us proudly. 'I've been taking her to dog-training classes all through the summer holidays.'

'Look, Freya *is* here,' Katy pointed out. Freya, tall and slim in her favourite purple tracksuit, was standing on the pitch where the Under-Thirteens always trained. Bouncing a football casually from one hand to the other, she was chatting to a woman we'd never seen before. As tall as Freya, this woman was even slimmer, almost bony. She had a serious, thin face and her long dark hair was plaited into dreadlocks decorated with green, red and yellow beads.

'Who's that?' Jasmin whispered. 'She looks a bit scary!'

At that moment Freya turned and noticed us.

'Girls, good to see you back,' she declared. But, it was odd. I noticed straightaway that she looked very uncomfortable and that puzzled me. Freya loved the start of the new season as much as we did, so why was she looking as if she wished she was a thousand miles away? Was it something to do with the stranger standing next to her? I stared at the woman suspiciously.

'Before we make a start, I'd like to introduce you to Ria Jones,' Freya continued. 'Ria's a coach, too.' Ria kind of half-smiled at us for about a second, then looked quite stern again. I didn't know who she was, but I'd started disliking her a little already. My mum always used to say that I made my mind up about people too quickly, but this Ria honestly *didn't* look very friendly.

'OK, girls, I need to talk to you…' Freya was looking and sounding even more anxious. I glanced sideways at Hannah who was nearby, and she raised her eyebrows at me. I knew that Hannah was thinking exactly the same thing as I was. *I've never seen Freya like this before…*

'I have some news for you,' Freya went on. 'You know my husband Tom is an engineer?' We all nodded. 'Well, he's been unexpectedly sent to Dubai for work. He'll be there for a couple of years, and I'm going with him. At the end of this week, actually.'

She indicated the woman standing next to her.

'So after tonight, Ria will be coaching the Under-Thirteens from now on.'

CHAPTER TWO

There was a stunned silence. I couldn't speak. I felt as if someone had just punched me in the guts very hard. It was a familiar, horrible feeling of pain and loss that I'd experienced before, and I hated it.

'Freya, you're kidding, right?' Jasmin cried. I glanced at her and saw tears in her eyes.

'I'm afraid not, Jasmin,' Freya said gently. 'It's all happened so suddenly, that it's taken me by surprise, too. But this is a big opportunity for Tom, and we felt he couldn't turn it down...'

She let her voice trail away uncomfortably, and silence fell again. All our excitement, all our passion, all our high spirits had just drained away in seconds, like someone had pulled out a plug. I bit my lip. I felt like I'd been on top of the world, soaring through the clouds, and someone had pulled me cruelly back down to earth with a bump.

'I can't believe it,' Hannah muttered in my ear. I didn't reply. I couldn't.

'We'll miss you, Freya,' Katy said a bit shakily. 'But good luck with the move.'

Then the others joined in, crowding around Freya and wishing her all the best. Except me. I stayed where I was. Memories were rushing through my head. My early training sessions with the Stars when I was eight, and Freya deciding I would make a good goalie. I didn't want to be a goalie, I wanted to be a star striker, I'd told her sulkily. Freya had asked me to go in goal for just one match, and from then on, I was hooked. I remembered Freya telling me off soundly over the years when I took too many risks or lost my temper on the pitch. Praising me to the skies when I made a fantastic save or stopped a penalty. Visiting me at home after Mum died…

I swallowed, my throat stinging. I don't cry, ever, unless I'm on my own. And I wouldn't cry now. But I was full of tears inside.

'Right, girls, let's get on with the training session,' Freya said briskly, looking a little damp around the eyes herself. 'The best send-off you can give me is to get down to training and push for promotion this year. I'll be keeping in touch with the club – and with you all too, I hope! – and I shall want to hear that you're challenging for the top.' She turned to Ria. 'I know Ria has big plans for the team. She's a fantastic coach.'

I glanced at Ria who allowed herself a small smile and no more. What *was* it with this woman? Did she think her face would crack or something? I scowled darkly at the thought that she would now be our new coach, bossing us around and telling us what to do. Ria looked like she would enjoy that.

Unfortunately, Ria saw me frowning at her and she frowned back slightly. Like I cared!

'OK, slow jog,' Freya called. She walked over and put her hand briefly on my shoulder before turning away. 'And make sure you shake your arms loose, too. Let's get going. We've wasted enough time.'

'I just can't believe it!' Hannah said again, as the team began to jog around the outside of the pitch. 'This is the *pits*.'

'And we were *sooo* happy!' Jasmin sighed. 'Ooh,

sorry!' she gasped, as she got a bit too close to Lauren in front and clipped her heels. 'I'm so upset, I don't know what I'm doing. I just love Freya to *bits*.'

'It's OK, Jas,' Lauren called over her shoulder. 'I know how you feel. It's *such* a downer that she's leaving when we'd psyched ourselves up for promotion and all.'

'We can still get promotion,' Katy pointed out, her sensible head on. 'That's really down to us.'

'Katy's right,' Grace said. 'Let's not get carried away here, guys. I'm as gutted as all of you that Freya's leaving, but who knows? Maybe Ria's a brilliant coach, too. We might learn a lot from her—'

'Like what, Little Miss Sunshine?' I scoffed rudely. I didn't mean to sound quite so sharp, but Grace was getting up my nose with her *be positive* attitude. 'She looks like a miserable old bag to me. She's hardly cracked a smile since she got here.'

'Georgie!' Jasmin giggled. 'Don't be like that. We've got to give Ria a *chance*.'

Why? I thought, but I didn't say it.

'I guess Grace could have a point.' Hannah waggled her arms vigorously as we jogged. 'Sometimes having a change shakes everything up and makes you see things differently.'

'Yes, I've noticed that,' Katy agreed with her own positive spin on the situation. God, why were they doing this? It made me *sick*. They obviously hadn't realised that things changing meant unhappiness and heartache and losing all the people you cared about. 'We'll just have to wait and see what Ria's like.'

'And then you'll find out I'm right.' I tried to keep my voice jokey because I was concerned about how upset, angry and anxious I was, deep inside. I didn't want the others to realise how bad I was feeling. 'Remember Martha the Misery, one of our coaches on the intensive training course last season? Well, Ria is going to be much, *much* worse—'

Jasmin suddenly burst out into a loud coughing fit which was so fake, it wouldn't have fooled a five-year-old. I glanced round and saw that Ria had come up silently behind us and was jogging along between Jasmin and Katy. She stared me straight between the eyes as if she expected me to apologise, but I didn't. Giving a tiny shrug, I turned round again and speeded up.

'*Slow* jog, Georgie!' Freya yelled as I pulled away from the others. I slowed down reluctantly. I felt so full of frustration and unhappiness that I could have run about ten miles straight off.

After we'd warmed up, Ria stood aside and watched us in silence as we did some agility training and practised running and turning with the ball, and controlled heading. Then I went in goal and the others took it in turns to take shots from different parts of the penalty box. Grace blasted a shot past me, so I picked the ball out of the net and booted it to Jo-Jo, who was next in line. Unfortunately I sliced it a bit and the ball spun off the pitch, heading straight towards Ria's head.

Everyone burst out laughing as Ria ducked smartly and the ball sailed over her. Everyone except Ria, that is. She straightened up and eyeballed me.

'I hope that was an accident, Georgie?' she asked coolly.

'Absolutely,' I agreed. 'I wasn't aiming at you. Not that time anyway.'

Freya gave me a sharp look, then glanced at her watch. 'OK, time to cool down, girls. Don't rush off at the end, though. I want to talk to you before you get changed.'

When we'd finished stretching and cooling down, Ria strolled over to Freya and shook hands with her. 'I'll be off now, then. Good luck with the move, Freya.' She looked round at everyone, ending with me. 'I'll see you all on Thursday then, girls.' Was it my imagination, or could I see a hint of a challenge in her stare? 'Bye for now.'

'Well done, girls,' Freya said warmly, as Ria walked away. 'That was an excellent session to finish on. You've got *such* a great chance to grab promotion this year. You're making me wish I wasn't leaving!'

'Don't, then,' I said, only half-jokingly.

Freya smiled at me, but didn't say anything. She walked over to the side of the pitch and picked up her rucksack.

'Just a little goodbye present, girls,' she said, beginning to hand out brightly-wrapped parcels.

I kept my head down as I tore off the purple tissue-paper. Freya had given us each some chocolate football boots.

'Thanks, Freya.' Jasmin gave her a big hug, and Lauren and some of the others did the same, but I couldn't. I'm not a huggy, touchy-feely type person, remember?

'Now, I'm warning you lot – keep in touch!' Freya said as we all walked back to the changing-room. 'I shall be dying to know what's happening every match-day, and I'll expect lots of emails from you all. OK? Promise?'

'We promise!' Hannah said earnestly, and the others agreed. Then there were more hugs and more goodbyes. I stayed quiet and apart, wanting to slip away without being noticed. I *hate* goodbyes. But I wasn't quick enough to get to the doors first, and Freya caught my arm as I tried to sidle past her.

'Wait a minute, Georgie. You wanted to speak to me after training, didn't you?'

I stared blankly at her.

'I had a text from you,' Freya reminded me, as the other girls went inside.

'Oh. That.' I shrugged. 'It doesn't matter now you're leaving…'

'Georgie.' Freya fixed me with her direct stare. She never let me get away with anything. *I was really going to miss her.* 'Tell me.'

'It's just that Melfield United are holding an Open Day at their stadium in three weeks' time,' I explained reluctantly. 'It's for charity, and Adey's helping to organise it. He asked me if some of the Springhill Stars teams could get involved somehow. Maybe put on some exhibition matches against the Melfield United Girls' teams, or run a stall or something. The money raised is going to the hospice that looked after Mum…' My voice trailed away. 'Anyway, like I said, it doesn't matter now you're leaving.'

'Of course it matters,' Freya said briskly. 'Things aren't going to grind to a halt just because I'm not here. The Open Day's for a good cause and it's a great opportunity for the club to showcase the teams and try to recruit some new players. I'll tell Ria and the other coaches. I'm sure they'd all like to be involved.'

I was silent. I wished I hadn't said anything now. The idea of Ria doing *anything* with the team just got right up my nose.

'Ria's a good coach, Georgie,' Freya remarked quietly as she opened the outer door for me. 'Just remember that.'

'I didn't say she wasn't,' I muttered. But Freya always did have an uncanny ability to read my mind. And as I trudged down the corridor to the changing-room, I knew that Freya knew that things had already got off to a bad start between me and Ria...

Wednesday 9th – 5pm

B-O-R-I-N-G day at school today. I'd forgotten my maths homework so I got a telling-off from Miss

Burton. All Hannah, Grace and Katy wanted to talk about was Freya leaving, and we kept on getting text messages from Jasmin and Lauren throughout the day, too. I don't think any of us did any work at all!

Grace was really getting on my nerves today. She kept going on and on *again* about how change can be good for us because it makes us see the world differently, and some such airy-fairy rubbish. She kept looking at me while she was saying it, too. Honestly, that girl is *so* sweet and nice and kind, it's almost sickening! She hasn't got a clue.

I don't mean that, really. I think Grace is ace (ha ha, I'm a poet and I didn't know it!).

I just wish Grace could see that life isn't all sweetness and light, and there sometimes is a downside. I can see a BIG, FAT DOWNSIDE RIGHT NOW, and she's called RIA.

Anyway, the others are coming over to my place tonight. We had to beg and plead with our parents to allow us to meet up, because they *totally* hate it if we want to get together on a school night. But we had a really good excuse this time. Because we didn't know that Freya was leaving, we didn't even have a prezzie and a card for her. So we're going to decide what we can get for Freya before she flies off to Dubai on Saturday.

I just hope Grace doesn't start her 'everything's wonderful and fantastic' routine again, or I might get extremely violent!

'So, any ideas?' Hannah looked enquiringly round at the rest of us as we lay sprawled on the old but comfy sofas in our living room. 'We can't let Freya go without giving her *something*.'

'Actually, maybe it'd be better if we didn't get her anything after all,' Jasmin chimed in. She had Rainbow on her lap, and he was purring gently in his sleep. 'My mum met Freya in the post office this morning, and Freya told her that they weren't taking much with them to Dubai, and they were having to put almost everything in storage.'

'So even if we got her something, she might have to leave it behind,' Grace mused.

'What about if we just make Freya a really special card?' I suggested. 'A card wouldn't take up much space in her luggage. We could stick a team photo on the front.'

'And we could all write our own messages inside,' Lauren said.

'Fab idea,' Hannah agreed. 'Shall we use the official team photo?'

'Nah, let's not,' I said. 'It's a bit prim and proper, isn't it, all of us sitting there in a row? How about someone brings a camera to training tomorrow and we take some fun shots and use one of those instead?'

The others nodded.

'I'll borrow my dad's digital camera,' Lauren offered. 'I've got one of my own, but Dad's is better.'

'We'll have to get Ria's permission,' Grace added. 'I'm sure she won't mind, though.'

'I bet she does,' I muttered under my breath. No one heard me, except Grace, because she was sitting right next to me. She glanced sharply in my direction, but didn't say anything.

'It's going to be so strange tomorrow night,' Katy sighed, resting her chin on her hands. 'Ria being our coach, not Freya, I mean.'

'Yeah, it'll take time to get used to her.' Lauren began plaiting Hannah's long, chestnut-coloured hair. 'I hope she's not as grumpy as she looks.'

'Ria probably wants to get to know us first before she starts being all matey.' Grace stared at me and this time she forced me to meet her gaze. 'Don't you think so, Georgie?'

'How the hell do I know?' I retorted, a bit more rudely than I'd intended (story of my life – I have a big mouth!). 'She *could* be the strictest, most miserable coach in the entire football universe. End of.'

'Freya said Ria was a good coach,' Katy reminded me gently.

I shrugged.

'Look, Georgie, we're all sad that Freya's leaving,' Grace went on. 'But there's nothing we can do about it. Except try to get along with Ria.'

'I just don't think she's going to be half as good as Freya was!' I burst out. 'Freya was strict, yes, but she liked having a laugh and she was kind, too. She cared about us when we had...problems.' I thought about my mum briefly, and pushed the memory away.

'Georgie's right.' Having finished plaiting Hannah's hair, Lauren now moved on to Jasmin's. 'Ria's got a lot to live up to.'

'Well, we don't *know* her properly yet, do we?' Katy pointed out. 'She might turn out to be as fantastic as Freya was.'

'No chance.' I shook my head.

Grace looked at me levelly. 'Is it actually *Ria* you don't like, Georgie? Or would you feel the same about *anyone* who replaced Freya?'

I rolled my eyes. 'Oh God, Grace, not a lecture,

please!' I groaned. I didn't want to think about the right answer to the question she'd just asked me. The trouble with Grace is that she's known me too long...

'Sometimes things have to change, Georgie,' Katy broke in, her big brown eyes serious. 'And then we just have to get on with it.' I wondered if she was thinking about her family moving from Poland to the UK two or three years ago. She'd never talked about it much.

'Oh, let's not go over the top here.' I yawned deliberately, wanting to avoid everything getting too emotional. I was feeling anxious enough, without the girls adding to it. 'I'm just keeping an open mind about whether Ria is going to be a good coach, that's all.'

'Are you sure you haven't made your mind up already, Georgie?' Grace asked softly. I was lost for words for a minute. *Why couldn't Grace just leave it?*

But before I could think of anything to say, the door burst open and Luke and Jack strolled in. I don't think I'd ever been so pleased to see them in my *life*.

'Hey, it's the Purple Petunias.' Jack nudged Luke

and they both started chuckling.

'Look, it's the Green Goblins,' Lauren shot back, quick as a flash, noting the dark green school sweatshirts the boys were wearing. The six of us collapsed into raucous giggles.

'What's happening, girls?' Luke asked, trying to be all cool and superior, but turning slightly red. 'Having a team meeting to talk about shoes, are we?'

'Actually, we were discussing why Georgie's so cool and clever, and why the rest of her family are so *weird*,' Jasmin said. 'But I've just realised that your dad is lovely, and so is Adey.' She gave my brothers a sweet, wide-eyed smile. 'So I guess that just leaves you two, then.'

I roared with laughter and the others joined in. Jack and Luke looked a bit taken aback. The girls had been round to ours a few times before, but Jack and Luke had both been out on those occasions, and they hadn't really met them all properly, until now. They *definitely* hadn't realised how much of a solid gang we were – and how full-on we could be when we were all together!

I saw Luke sneaking looks at Grace. I'd noticed it before, the last time she came round. The girls are all pretty and striking in their own way (I'm not including ME in that statement, by the way!), but Grace with her model looks always stood out. I was pleased to see that Grace didn't look at all impressed with Luke and Jack.

'We need to discuss tactics for Saturday's match now.' I got up and pointedly held the door open. 'So why don't you run along and find something else to do, like good little boys?'

'Tactics?' Jack snorted in disgust. 'Like, what colour nail varnish to wear?' And he and Luke started grinning like idiots, pretending to paint each other's nails and fluttering their eyelashes.

'Maybe you could recommend one?' Grace said, raising her eyebrows. 'As you seem to be such experts.'

The look on Luke's and Jack's faces was priceless. I hustled them out before they had time to react, and shut the door.

'Thanks, guys,' I said, still smiling. 'Those two drive me *nuts*.'

'Oh, but they don't really *mean* all that stuff about girls and football, do they?' Jasmin said with a grin. She glanced out of the window as a car drew up outside. 'There's my mum. We'd better go, Lauren.' She scooped Rainbow gently off her lap and put him down on the sofa. Rainbow purred a little louder, but didn't open his eyes.

'Yes, they're just teasing, aren't they?' Grace agreed, as her dad arrived to take her, Hannah and Katy home. 'Don't let it get to you, Georgie.'

I forced a cheerful nod as I waved goodbye to them all. I would *never* let anyone see how much Luke and Jack sometimes hurt me with their comments. Not even the girls.

The funny thing is, I'd thought that we'd all pull together and become closer after Mum died. I was wrong...

Thursday 10th – 4.30pm

God, what a day. And it's not even over yet.

I had a really terrible time at school, because I was feeling all anxious and worried about training tonight and meeting Ria again. I flunked my maths test, even though I knew how to do all the algebra, and Miss Burton had a right go at me. I don't think I'm her favourite student at the moment...

And then Hannah, Katy and I spent ages at lunchtime, trying to cheer Grace up. She was really down, which isn't like her at all, but she told us that her mum and dad had had an argument this morning over breakfast, and that she and Gemma had taken sides and they'd ended up having a row too. So all in all, not a great day.

But when I got home, things suddenly got even worse. Dad and Adey were waiting for me. Adey was holding Rainbow in his arms, and Rainbow's eyes were open, but he wasn't moving or making a sound.

Dad told me that Rainbow had collapsed in the garden next door, and Mrs Wasim had come rushing round to tell us. We're just waiting for Jack and Luke to get home from school, and then we're all going to the vet's. I did suggest to Dad that we could go straightaway without the boys, but he shook his head. He didn't say anything, but I guessed he thinks that Rainbow isn't going to make it, so we should all be there to say goodbye.

But I don't want to believe that. Rainbow was Mum's cat. She loved him, and he's one of the few links we still have left with Mum.

I don't want Rainbow to die.

CHAPTER THREE

'I'll leave you to say your goodbyes to Rainbow.' The vet glanced sympathetically at us and then left the little room, closing the door without a sound.

I stared at a calendar with pictures of fluffy pets that hung on the wall opposite me. September's picture was two white kittens with big green eyes, sitting in a patch of sunflowers. As I gazed at the calendar, I was reciting the nine times table in my head. I've discovered in the past that it helps me hold back tears when I *really* want to cry.

Eventually I forced myself to look down at the examining-table. Rainbow lay on a blue blanket, perfectly still, his breathing rapid and shallow, eyes closed. Adey was stroking his ears. Jack and Dad stood staring down at Rainbow, their faces closed and shuttered. Meanwhile, Luke was pacing around the room like a caged tiger. He didn't look at the table.

'Goodbye, old boy,' Adey murmured.

Jack gave Rainbow a swift pat and then went over to stand and look out of the window. I couldn't see his face. I waited until Dad had tickled Rainbow's chin, and then I went and put my face very close and nuzzled the fluffy black fur around his ears.

'Bye, Rainbow,' I whispered, so low that no one else could hear me. 'I love you loads.'

Luke looked jumpy and nervous. He stroked Rainbow's head quickly, and then went to stand with Jack at the window. They avoided looking at each other. I guessed that everyone was thinking about Mum, too, as well as Rainbow. I know I was. Then, a few minutes later, the vet came in.

'You can stay with him, if you like,' she offered gently. 'It's very quick, and he won't suffer.'

We didn't want to leave Rainbow all alone at the end, so Adey stayed while the vet gave Rainbow the injection. The rest of us went out into the waiting-room. None of us spoke. I felt like if I started crying, I'd never stop.

'Oh well,' Luke muttered, 'maybe I can get a dog now?'

'*God!*' I burst out furiously. 'Do you *ever* take *anything* seriously at all?'

'Georgie,' Dad said, putting his arm around me. All the people in the waiting-room holding cat baskets and dog leads and cardboard pet carriers turned to stare at us.

'I only meant—' Luke began, 'I just – oh, forget it!' And he slouched out of the room into the car park. Jack went after him.

Dad cleared his throat. 'Georgie, don't you remember how Luke was always asking your mum if he could have a dog when he was younger?' he said quietly. 'It turned into a kind of running joke between them, your mum always saying that Rainbow would leave home if we got a puppy. I think Luke was just trying to lighten us up a little...'

'Well, it wasn't funny,' I muttered, my eyes stinging. My throat was raw, too, from trying to hold back my tears. I just wanted to fling myself into my dad's arms and *howl*. The combination of Rainbow's death and talking about Mum was a killer. We did sometimes talk about Mum, and her photos were still all over the house, but it wasn't *easy*. My dad's brilliant and a great laugh most of the time, but he's not too good with the emotional stuff. Mum used to do most of that.

Adey came out, then. His eyes were red-rimmed, and he was carrying the empty cat basket. I swallowed and looked away.

The three of us trooped outside without a word and joined Jack and Luke, who were leaning against our car. We drove home in silence until Dad said suddenly, 'Georgie, are you going to your training session tonight?'

I shrugged and glanced at my watch. 'I might as well,' I replied, thinking that a bit of footie would stop me brooding about everything that had happened today. 'I'll be late, but Freya won't mind when I explain—'

I stopped abruptly. Freya wouldn't be there, would she? Ria was our coach now.

The thought of having to cope with someone new, especially someone like Ria, was almost too much, the way I was feeling. I wondered whether to change my mind, but we'd pulled up outside the house now, and Dad turned to me.

'Pop inside and pick up your kit, love, and I'll take you straight there.'

I hesitated, but the thought of seeing Lauren, Katy and the others swung it. I knew they'd rally round me when I told them about Rainbow.

I dived into the house and grabbed my stuff. I hadn't packed my sports bag after school like I usually did because I was too worried about Rainbow, and I couldn't find my footie boots *anywhere*. Eventually, steaming with impatience, I discovered them kicked into a corner behind my bedroom door.

'At last,' Dad said as I hurtled into the car again. 'I was about to send out a search party.'

I glanced at my watch again and groaned. I should be in the changing-room and getting ready for training *right now*.

Dad drove like a hero, but we kept hitting every red light, the way you always do when you're in a hurry. When we pulled into the college car park, I leapt out of the car and ran for it.

'I'll be back to pick you up,' Dad called after me.

I sprinted down the college corridors, getting some disapproving looks from people who'd arrived to do their flower-arranging or Beginners Italian or belly-dancing evening classes or whatever. When I reached the back of the college, I saw Hannah, Lauren, Grace, Jasmin and Katy standing outside the door of the changing-room, looking anxiously up and down the corridor.

'There she is!' Jasmin yelled.

'God, Georgie, talk about living dangerously!' Lauren grinned as I dashed up to them. 'We thought you weren't coming. Jo-Jo and the others have already gone outside.'

Hannah was looking at my face. 'What's wrong, Georgie?' she asked.

'We had to go to the vet's after school,' I said, trying to hold myself together. 'Rainbow collapsed. He had some sort of stroke.'

'No!' Jasmin's eyes were round with horror.

'What did the vet say?' Lauren wanted to know.

'Is he OK?' asked Grace.

I shook my head. I didn't trust myself to speak.

'Oh, Georgie!' Jasmin clapped her hand to her mouth. 'But he was *fine* yesterday. He sat on my lap!'

'I'm so sorry, Georgie.' Katy put her arm around me. So did Hannah, and the others drew closer, too.

'It's OK, honestly,' I muttered, trying to convince myself as much as anyone else. 'Rainbow was really old, and it was quick and painless, so—' I broke off before I started sobbing and totally disgraced myself. 'I'd better get changed.'

I thought the girls might leave me on my own and go to join Jo-Jo, Ruby and the others. But they didn't. They all filed back into the empty changing-room with me and stood around as I wriggled out of my school uniform.

'Did anyone ask Ria about the photo for Freya's card?' I slipped my sweatshirt over my head and glanced enquiringly at the others.

'I did, and she said yes,' Hannah replied. 'But we have to do it at the end of training.'

'My dad's camera's in my locker,' said Lauren, rolling her eyes heavenwards. 'It took me *ages* to persuade him to let me borrow it, and I'm not even going to *tell* you how much he paid for it. I just hope I can get it home in one piece.'

'Better hope no one breaks into our lockers while we're training and nicks it then,' Jasmin said mischievously. Lauren turned pale.

'Don't!' she groaned. 'I'd be grounded for six months.'

At that moment I glanced up from lacing my boots and I saw Ria standing in the doorway. She didn't look very amused.

'Girls, you should have been outside five minutes ago,' she remarked coolly. Her gaze flicked to me. 'Especially as you're all ready except for Georgie.'

'Sorry,' Grace, Hannah, Lauren and Katy said together, and Jasmin gave Ria an apologetic, toothy grin. But she did not smile back.

'I expect my teams to be punctual,' Ria went on. 'Training only lasts an hour, and if you're late arriving, you're missing out.'

She was *definitely* eyeballing me now, but I still didn't say sorry. I wasn't in the mood to be messed about.

'Well, why are we wasting time hanging around here, then?' I said breezily, jumping to my feet. I marched past Ria and out of the changing-room.

I thought she might say something, but she didn't. I speeded up and ran out onto the pitch to join Alicia, Ruby and the others who were aimlessly kicking a ball about. The other Stars teams had already started their training sessions – it was just the Under-Thirteens who hadn't begun yet.

Ria joined us, the other girls scurrying along behind her. They looked a bit anxious, while Ria was definitely irritated. I could tell that Jasmin,

Lauren and the others were worried that I was going to go into naughty little devil mode.

Behave yourself, whispered the Georgie angel on my shoulder. *Just enjoy your football, like you always do.*

Don't let her get away with treating you badly, whispered the Georgie devil in my other ear. *She's got to prove she's a good coach, like Freya, before you even start to like her.*

'Right, gather round,' Ria called, glancing very pointedly at her watch. 'We can finally make a start. OK, girls, firstly I want you to know that I'm very excited about taking over your team.'

I rolled my eyes. Ria looked about as excited as someone being offered a plate of roadkill for dinner.

'I know that Freya had been with the club for a long time, and you're all going to miss her. But sometimes it's a good thing to have a change—'

Oh please. Not the 'change is good' lecture again.

'—and I'm sure we're going to make a great team, when we've got to know each other a little better.' Ria looked round at us all, and, yes, once again I got *the* stare. 'Just keep in mind that we all want the same thing – a good run in the County Cup, and promotion to the top league. Now, let's stretch those

54

muscles and get warmed up.'

Ria started us off with jogging and high knees, then skipping forwards, backwards and sideways. Nothing too controversial there, then. But the way she *stared* at us so critically really annoyed me. It was almost as if she was determined to search for all our little faults and highlight them, just to show that she was a better coach than Freya. And she kept on looking at *me*. I knew I wasn't joining in with as much enthusiasm as I usually did, but it wasn't deliberate, honest. My legs felt like they were filled with lead, and half of my mind was still back at the vet's with poor old Rainbow...

'No slacking, Georgie!' Ria yelled, frowning. 'Knees higher!'

I muttered a rude word under my breath. Ria's frown deepened. Maybe she could lip-read. I didn't care. I thought about slowing down deliberately, just to annoy her, but before I could do anything, Grace and Katy came up one on either side of me.

'Are you two policing me?' I asked crossly.

'Yes,' Grace replied, patting my arm. 'Don't do something you'll regret later, Georgie.'

'Who says I'll regret anything?' I retorted, speeding up to get away from them. Unfortunately,

I could see that Ria thought I was now trying to impress her, so I slowed down again, so suddenly that Ruby and Emily bumped into the back of me. Everyone started laughing, except Ria. Little devil Georgie was definitely in charge tonight...

Despite being on edge because of Ria, the feel of a ball at my feet began to work its magic. Although I loved being a goalie, I still enjoyed practising the skills that the other girls were learning, like volleying, heading and chipping the ball. Freya said it was good for me to know what I was facing when I was in goal. But she also used to try and give me a bit of specialised training between the posts every so often, or one of the other coaches would sometimes get all the goalies from the different teams to practise together. I loved trying out different ways to save a shot – although I hadn't had the nerve yet to try out the 'scorpion kick'. If you don't know what *that* is, check it out on the internet. You won't believe your eyes. (The goalie's hairstyle is worth checking out too!)

Anyway, I calmed down a bit, although Ria was still getting on my nerves with her poker-faced attitude. She criticised me once or twice, and I had to bite back the retort that sprang to my lips. I could see the girls watching me a bit anxiously. Then Ria told us to get into pairs, and I saw Grace flick a meaningful glance at the others and head straight towards me. I knew what *her* little game was so I immediately grabbed Jasmin's arm.

'Be my partner, Jas,' I said.

'Cool,' Jasmin said cheerfully, having completely missed, in her usual dippy way, what Grace was intending – which was to keep *me* out of trouble.

We started off. One of us had to toss the ball underarm to the other player, who was supposed to volley it back. The person who was throwing the ball had to keep moving forwards, forcing the volleying player to move backwards all the time. It was quite difficult.

I was first up for volleying and got four out of six of Jasmin's throws pretty well nailed. Then it was Jasmin's turn.

'I hate volleying,' Jasmin muttered as I tossed the ball to her. She stuck her foot out and hit the ball more by luck than anything else, I think! I caught it neatly.

'That was good,' I said encouragingly, moving forwards and throwing the ball to her again.

Unfortunately, Jasmin forgot to move backwards.

She gave a shriek as the ball flew towards her, too close, and she tried to jump back. She couldn't keep her balance and stay upright, and she fell over backwards like a slow-motion film.

'Help!' Jasmin gasped as she hit the deck, legs in the air.

Almost helpless with laughter – and believe me, that felt good after the day I'd just had – I ran over and hauled her to her feet. As Jasmin struggled to get up, though, she caught her foot in the leg of her shorts and pulled them halfway down, giving me and everyone else a great view of her bright pink knickers.

By this time I was in hysterics. So was Jasmin and everyone else around us, including Grace and the others.

'Jasmin! Georgie!' Ria called. I glanced round to see if she was smiling, but what a surprise – she wasn't. 'Get back to work, please.'

'Oh, lighten up, you sour-faced old dragon,' I said, a *bit* more loudly than I'd intended.

I thought Ria would go mad at me. But she didn't.

'Stay behind at the end, Georgie,' was all she said, and very quietly, too. 'I want to talk to you.'

'*Georgie!*' Hannah groaned as Ria went over to

Jo-Jo and Ruby. 'What did you do *that* for?'

'Because she's getting on my nerves,' I retorted, picking up our ball. My mood had gone flat again. 'She must have had an operation to remove her sense of humour.'

'Sorry, Georgie.' Jasmin looked distressed. 'That was all *my* fault.'

'No, it's all Ria's fault,' I assured her. 'She couldn't crack a smile if her life depended on it.'

'I'm with Georgie on this one,' Lauren said, slinging her arm round my shoulders. 'I don't like you-know-who one bit, either. She's *s-o-o-o* different to Freya.'

'Georgie, have you ever thought that Ria might be nervous about taking this job on?' Grace suggested with a smile. 'She might lighten up later.'

'Or maybe she *is* just a sour-faced old dragon,' Jasmin suggested solemnly. 'You know what? I'm scared of her!'

'GIRLS!' yelled the sour-faced old dragon. 'Get back to work, please!'

We carried on with the training session. When we finished the volleying practice and moved onto the next drill, I noticed Grace having a quiet word with Ria, over to one side and out of earshot of everyone else. I even saw Ria glance across at me, although I didn't think anything of it. It was only later that I found out what Grace had been up to.

At the end of the training session, Lauren ran to fetch her dad's camera and we took some photos for Freya's card. We messed around, having a great laugh, taking action shots of us booting footballs around and putting the traffic cones we dribble around on our heads, like witches' hats. Ria hung back quietly, keeping an eye on us as she packed up our equipment.

'I'll choose the best ones, stick them on an email and send them out to you all when I get home.' Lauren switched off the camera. 'Then we can vote on the one for the card.'

'Great stuff,' said Emily. 'Should one of us text Freya, and ask if we can go round and see her tomorrow to hand the card over?'

'Grace, you do that,' I said, as we wandered off the pitch in one big crowd. 'You're the captain, which makes it kind of more official!'

Grace grinned and nodded.

'Georgie,' Ria called from behind us.

'Oh, *bum*!' I muttered under my breath. I'd forgotten that Ria had asked me to stay behind, *obviously* to give me a good telling-off.

'Do you need a lift home, Georgie?' asked Hannah. 'My mum won't mind. I can hang on and wait for you.'

I shook my head. 'My dad's coming for me,' I said. 'You go, guys.' I drew my finger slowly across my throat. 'I'm in for it now.'

Giving me sympathetic looks, the others said goodbye and went off to the changing-room. I turned back to find Ria waiting for me.

'Shall we get something straight right away, Georgie?' she said in a quiet, even tone. 'I know you were very fond of Freya, but I'm in charge of the team now. And I expect you to knuckle down and get on with it without being either rude or disobedient. If you don't want me as your coach, you always have the option of leaving and joining another team. Is that clear?'

'Yep,' I muttered.

Do what she says, little angel Georgie instructed me. *Otherwise she could make life difficult for you.*

Don't let her boss you around, whispered little devil Georgie. *You don't like her, so let her know it. Maybe then* she'll *be the one leaving and joining another team!*

61

'By the way,' Ria went on, 'I was sorry to hear about your cat. That must have upset you, so we won't say any more about your behaviour tonight.'

I gawped at her in complete disbelief. Then the penny dropped. *Grace!*

'The other thing I wanted to mention was that Freya told me about the Open Day at the Melfield United ground. She said it was particularly important to you that the Stars took part?' Ria raised an eyebrow at me, but I kept silent. I was no way going to mention anything about Mum and raising money for the hospice. Anyway, Freya had probably already told her the details.

'I'm going to be discussing it with the other coaches this weekend, but I just wanted to let you know I'm sure the club will get involved one way or another,' Ria said briskly.

I was completely wrong-footed. I was just about to mumble a reluctant thank you, but Ria forestalled me.

'Oh, I also meant to say earlier that we definitely need to sort out some specialised goalie training for you, Georgie,' she said thoughtfully. 'The stuff you're doing with the outfield players is useful, but I think we should concentrate more on intensive goalkeeping coaching.'

'I *like* training with the others,' I butted in – OK, I admit it, *rudely.*

'We'll see,' was all Ria replied. But she might as well have come right out and said *I'm the coach, and what I say goes, so get on with it or you'll regret it.* Because I could hear all that and more in the tone of her voice. Didn't I get any say in this at all?

By now I was *boiling* with fury inside. Freya had been strict too, yes, but she'd always been open to discussion. Ria was just a grim, humourless old dragon who didn't seem to have a likeable bone in her whole body!

I spun round and marched off to the changing-room without saying goodbye, head held high.

'Georgie,' I heard Ria call from behind me. 'Didn't you forget something?'

I turned back reluctantly. Ria pointed to my Stars tracksuit top which I'd flung off when I warmed up. It was lying at the far side of the pitch. So much for my big exit!

Keeping my eyes down, I stomped across the grass. Meanwhile, Ria disappeared into the college with the bag of footballs. I grabbed my top and then went back to the changing-room. Everyone had gone except for Alicia and Debs, and they were just on their way out as I went in.

'Did Ria chew your ears off, Georgie?' Debs asked.

'Oh, you know me,' I replied breezily. 'Water off a duck's back. What do you guys think of her, anyway?'

Alicia's round, friendly face creased into a fearsome scowl. 'She's a bit full-on, isn't she?'

'Alicia's scared of her,' Debs said with a grin.

'Ooh, I am not!' Alicia poked her in the ribs.

'Don't worry, Ali,' I said, opening my locker. 'So's Jasmin! See you Saturday.'

The thought of the first match of the season, against the Fairmount Foxes, sent a burst of adrenalin zipping through me as Alicia and Debs left, shouting goodbye. Once we were on the pitch, I could ignore Ria. I'd be doing what I loved most – playing footie with all my mates. It would take my mind off poor old Rainbow, too...

I stripped off and jumped back into my school uniform. My sweatshirt was covered in cat hairs, and the sight of them gave me an unpleasant jolt. Maybe I'd been a bit hard on Luke when we were at the vet's, I thought guiltily. But then, he was always being hard on me, wasn't he? So I pushed the thought firmly away.

I was really late by the time I left the changing-room. Dad would have had a long wait out in the car park. He usually brought the evening paper with him to read while he waited, though, because he knew that our gang of six were often last to leave because we were chattering so much!

But when I ran out of the college tonight, Dad wasn't reading his paper. He wasn't even in the car. He was standing in the car park, deep in discussion with someone.

RIA!

My heart flipped over a few times and then sank down into my Nike trainers. I knew Ria was complaining about me, I just knew it! She hadn't wasted a minute, had she?

Just then Dad glanced up and saw me. He smiled.

'So there you are, gorgeous. Ready to go?'

I nodded, glancing warily at Ria. Had she been complaining about me or hadn't she? Judging from Dad's reaction, it didn't *seem* like it.

'Nice to meet you, Mr Taylor,' Ria said, shaking hands with my dad. Then her gaze switched to me, and I could read the challenge in it. 'I'll see you at the match on Saturday, Georgie.'

Oh, she was clever! In that moment, I realised

exactly what Ria was up to. She was letting me know that by getting my dad on-side, she had another way to keep me under control.

But what Ria didn't know was that little devil Georgie *loves* a challenge.

CHAPTER
FOUR

Thursday 10th – 8pm

Just got back home from training, and had some spaghetti that Adey made. We seem to live on pasta and takeaways! We've still got all Mum's recipe books, and sometimes I wonder if I should suggest trying something new. But then they might expect me to do all the cooking, just because I'm a girl, so I keep quiet!

The house seems so empty without Rainbow. Adey had moved his cat basket and food bowl before I got home, so at least I didn't have to look at them. I'm upstairs now, doing my homework – well, OK, writing in my diary first. That's much more important!

I had a good moan to Adey about Ria, but he just told me that part of being a good football player is learning to get along with your team-mates and your coach even if you don't really *like* them, for whatever reason. You have to see the big picture because it's all for the good of the team and blah, blah, blah. Now don't get me wrong, little angel Georgie can SEE that's he's absolutely right – but little devil Georgie can't see why she should just put up and shut up!

Lauren was really quick and had the pics from the training session loaded and emailed out to us not long after Dad and I got home. We've agreed on a brilliant photo of us all with our arms around each other.

I'm still a bit annoyed about Grace telling Ria (sour-faced old dragon or SFOD for short!) about Rainbow. I don't want Ria feeling sorry for me. That's typical of Grace, though – she's lovely, but she does like sticking her nose into other people's business. I wish she'd just butt out!

The sun was pouring through my bedroom window, the sky was blue, I was fizzing with excitement and it was Saturday! Our first match of the season was due to start in about an hour – YAY!

I could hardly wait, even though it wouldn't be the same without Freya. The whole team had gone round to her place yesterday evening to deliver the card. It was lucky she was in, as it was too big to go through the letterbox! It was really good to see her and say one last goodbye...

I'd packed my sports bag the night before, but I still unzipped it to take a peek, for maybe the millionth time. Footie boots – check. Springhill Stars shirt – check. Shorts – check. Baseball cap in case it was sunny—

My phone buzzed. I grabbed it and saw a message from Hannah.

Only 1 hr to go – hooray!!!

I grinned. Hannah had been texting me (and probably the others, too) a countdown to the match since 7.30 that morning.

I was about to chuck my phone back onto the bed when it rang. *Lauren* came up on the display, and I hit the answer button.

'Hey, you!' Lauren shrieked happily, almost deafening me. 'Oh, wait a minute, Georgie—'

I waited impatiently as Lauren began twittering away to someone standing next to her.

'Sorry about that,' she apologised breathlessly

a few minutes later. 'Tanya was asking me what I want for lunch.'

'Oh, God, the pressures of having a live-in housekeeper!' I teased. Now I could hear barking in the background.

'Chelsea, get down!' Lauren ordered. 'Who's a good girl, then?'

'Are you talking to me or the dog?' I asked.

'Sorry!' Lauren gasped again. 'Chelsea's dead excited. She always goes mad when I tie a purple ribbon to her collar because she knows it's match-day! Anyway, what was I ringing about?' Lauren went on distractedly.

'I have no idea,' I replied.

'Oh, yes!' Lauren said. 'I'm calling all the girls to ask how they're doing their hair today. I thought it would be cool if we all wore purple nail varnish and purple ribbons in our hair to match our shirts. So that we look alike.'

'Strange football fact number 567,' I said. 'At the 1998 World Cup, the whole of the Romanian team dyed their hair blonde before their match against Croatia.'

'Ooh, is that really true?' Lauren exclaimed. 'What a brilliant idea! Maybe we could dye ours purple?'

We both burst out laughing. 'Well, to be perfectly honest, I don't own a purple ribbon or a single bottle of nail varnish,' I said. 'But I guess you knew that already!'

'No problem, I'll bring a purple ribbon for you. And get to the college early so that I've got time to paint your nails.'

'No ribbons and definitely no nail varnish—' I began, but Lauren had already rung off.

I shook my head in amusement as I grabbed my bag. Girls' stuff like ribbons and nail varnish and make-up was a mystery to me. The others were well into it, though. Even Katy, who didn't have a lot of money, always had beautifully shiny straight hair and she often wore pretty little sparkly earrings or a thin silver chain around her neck. I guess I kind of envied their confidence with clothes and dressing-up just a bit…

But what on earth would Luke and Jack say if I started trying to glam up, I reminded myself. No, that kind of thing just wasn't *me* at all.

'Ready, Georgie?' Dad called up the stairs.

'You bet!' I yelled back, happiness surging through me as I raced for the door.

*

71

The raucous excitement in the changing-room was deafening when I finally arrived, after getting stuck in the Saturday morning shopping traffic (twice!). Not all of the club teams were playing at home today so the changing-room was only half-full, but the feeling of anticipation in the air set me tingling all over.

'Georgie!' Jasmin was leaping up and down in 'our' corner of the large room. Her long dark hair was tied up with a purple ribbon in an off-centre ponytail that bobbed madly as she waved at me. Meanwhile, Lauren was sitting on the bench, the tip of her tongue sticking out of her mouth as she concentrated on painting Katy's nails. Both of them were wearing purple scrunchies. 'You've *got* to join in!'

'Don't argue, Georgie,' added Grace, coming out of the loos at that exact moment. She was wearing a stretchy purple headband holding back her glossy blonde hair. 'Just do as you're told!'

I glanced round. Even Jo-Jo, Ruby and the others were all wearing purple in their hair and on their nails. At that moment the changing-room door flew open and Hannah waltzed in, beaming. Her long brown ponytail was tied up with a sparkly purple ribbon.

'Fab idea of yours, Lauren!' Hannah laughed, displaying her deep lilac fingernails. 'I hope you're doing it too, Georgie?'

'I can't wear my baseball cap if I've got a ribbon stuck on top of my head,' I pointed out. 'And I'll chip the nail varnish the second I have to save the ball.'

'I can see the thing about the nail varnish,' Lauren admitted, finishing off Katy's nails with a flourish. 'But...' She jumped to her feet, a wicked glint in her eyes. 'Whoever said you had to wear a ribbon in your *hair*?'

The other girls immediately surrounded me. I tried to fight back, but there were just too many of them! By the time they'd finished with me, I had two purple satin ribbons looped through my boot laces and knotted in bows on top.

'I look like a clown,' I grumbled, trying not to laugh.

'You look cute!' Jasmin giggled.

'Girls?'

We all turned to see Ria standing in the doorway. She looked us up and down, and then frowned.

'Just remember that this is the first and very important step in our campaign for promotion,' Ria

73

said in an ultra-serious voice. 'It's good to enjoy yourselves and boost team morale, but don't lose sight of the fact that you need to *concentrate* today. You're completely capable of winning this match, so I want to see you go out there and do it.'

And she turned round and walked away, leaving us all standing there with our mouths hanging open. It couldn't have been more different from Freya's encouraging, but light-hearted, pre-match talk.

'*Well!*' I gasped, rolling my eyes.

'That was a bit full-on, wasn't it?' Jasmin groaned, clutching my arm. 'She's *really* frightened me now!'

'I wish Ria would loosen up a bit,' Lauren complained. 'I bet even if we win the County Cup as well as promotion, she'll *still* have a face like she swallowed a lemon.'

'Come on, guys, let's forget about her,' Grace suggested, flinging her arms around Hannah and Katy. 'Let's try and win promotion for Freya, OK?'

'OK!' we all shouted enthusiastically. Alicia, Debs, Jo-Jo, Ruby and Emily joined us, and we had a team hug.

'Go, Springhill Stars!' Grace yelled.

Whooping and cheering we rushed for the door

and bounced down the corridor to the outside doors. My heart was thumping with excitement, and I couldn't keep a big smile off my face. I was grinning from ear to ear, and so were the others when I glanced over at them.

The brilliant sunshine warmed us as we went outside and ran to join the Fairmount Foxes on the pitch. As I positioned myself between the sticks so that the rest of the team could take a few practice shots, I checked where Dad was standing. He had his own favourite spot on the far side of the pitch near the halfway line, and I liked to wave at him every so often from my goalmouth. Sometimes he came with Adey, sometimes he stood with Jasmin's parents, or Grace's, but mostly he was on his own.

But today Dad *wasn't* alone. He was chatting to Mr and Mrs Bell, Lauren's parents. They had Chelsea with them, wearing a purple ribbon through her collar, and Mrs Bell looked impossibly glamorous, as usual, like she spent her whole life in a beauty salon. But standing next to Dad were two other people I instantly recognised...

'Aren't those your brothers, Georgie?' Katy asked, fixing me with that direct stare of hers.

She was right! Luke and Jack had turned up, right

out of the blue. *Oh my God!* I could not *believe* it. It was *years* since they'd been to one of my games. That was partly because they sometimes had a match to play themselves, for the school team – not always though, because those games were sometimes played mid-week after school had finished. They just hadn't bothered to come along even when they *were* free. But now here they were. A rush of happiness flooded through me. I had to admit that I *loved* the thought of Luke and Jack coming to watch me doing something that was so important to me. Maybe now they'd see me as a *person*, someone with hopes and dreams and feelings, and not just some annoying little sister they were always trying to wind up...

But wait a minute...

'Wake up, Georgie!' Ria yelled as Jasmin tapped a soft shot past me.

'Oh, shut up,' I muttered as I retrieved the ball from the back of the net. My brain was working overtime as I tried to figure out exactly why Luke and Jack had appeared, today of all days.

I groaned to myself. *Of course!* I knew that Luke had heard me complaining to Adey about Ria on Thursday night after training. He must have told

Jack, and they'd decided it would be good fun to come and wind me up even more at the game today, knowing that I wasn't getting along with Ria.

To my horror, I felt my throat close up as if I was going to start crying. Quickly I gave myself a mental shake. I wasn't going to let Ria *or* those two clowns ruin my game.

Clowns...

I glanced down at the two big purple bows on my boots as everyone got into position for kick-off. I bent over and swiftly wrenched the ribbons loose. No way was I going to give Luke or Jack any more ammunition to use against me!

'Eyes front, Georgie,' Ria called, as I turned to toss the ribbons into the back of my goal. 'Don't lose sight of the ball, *ever.*'

Could you be any more obvious? I wanted to yell back. Like I was going to stand with my back to the action! But I didn't say anything. I didn't want to have a slanging match with Ria in front of Luke and Jack. Or Dad. So I gritted my teeth and fixed my eyes on the ball as Grace kicked off.

The Fairmount Foxes had finished near the bottom of our league last season, and we'd been in the top half so, like Ria had said earlier, this was a match we were expecting to win. What none of us were expecting, though, was how much Ria was going to yell at us.

'Challenge for the ball, Jasmin!' Ria roared at the top of her lungs as Jasmin went in for the kill. She groaned loudly when Jas stumbled a little and missed the tackle. 'Stay with it – don't give up!'

And then, when Grace had a chance to take a shot, Ria was bawling at her from the minute she touched the ball. 'Go *on*, Grace! Take it to the left – the left! Watch out for the defender on your right!' And then she groaned loudly when Grace missed the goal by millimetres – probably because Ria had totally put her off!

'I didn't realise Ria was going to be so loud,' Hannah whispered to me as we gathered to defend a Foxes free kick just outside the penalty area. 'She's much more in-your-face than Freya was.'

'I know,' I agreed, adjusting the peak of my cap to block out the sun. 'It's a bit of a shock, isn't it, when she's been so serious and solemn up till now!'

'Makes a change from *you* yelling at us, though, doesn't it, Georgie?' Jasmin said with a little wink.

'Ho, ho, ho, very funny,' I retorted. I already told you that I have this big mouth, remember? And I do like to use it on match days! But I'd been so amazed by the change in Ria, that I'd hardly said *anything* so far. 'I haven't had a chance to get a word in edgeways today—'

'*Georgie!*' Ria called. 'Concentrate!'

I scowled. 'Who the hell does she think she is?' I muttered. 'Of course I'm going to concentrate!'

'Georgie, look out!' gasped Katy, who was defending alongside me.

The Foxes had sneakily stuck a couple of their players in our defensive wall, and they then nipped aside at the last minute to leave a hole. Their striker tried to blast the ball through the gap, but it was a fairly weak shot and I gathered it firmly in my arms.

Ria was yelling something again, but I ignored her. As the Foxes jogged out of my penalty area, I could see that Lauren, who hadn't come back to defend, was free and clear a little way along the right-hand side of the pitch. And if I could just pass the ball accurately to her, she'd be on for the break...

I think the Foxes were expecting me to take a goal kick. Instead I hurled the ball overarm straight towards Lauren.

Lauren was brilliant. I overthrew the ball slightly,

but she kept her eye on it and dashed forward, capturing it neatly as it fell. She had a slight struggle to keep it in play, but then she was off, racing down the wing like a greyhound.

'Fantastic!' Ria yelled. 'Keep going, Lauren!'

The Foxes only had one defender in their half, apart from the goalie, because everyone had come up to our end for the free kick. So they were all chasing back desperately, and Lauren was miles in front of them. She managed to get round the lone defender with one of the neat side-steps we'd learned at the Brazilian skills school. Then she homed in on the goal. I saw Lauren glance sideways and I knew she was looking to see if Grace was coming up alongside. Grace was our star striker and if anyone could score in this situation, it was her. But Grace was still a few yards behind, and there were two Fairmount defenders rushing right towards Lauren.

'DON'T HANG ABOUT, LAUREN!' I shrieked. 'SHOOT!'

I heard Ria yell *SHOOT!* at exactly the same moment as I did. As Lauren moved into the Foxes' penalty area, the goalie hesitated, wondering whether to come out or not – and that was her mistake. Lauren drove the ball past her where it nestled very satisfactorily in the far left-hand corner of the net.

'Goal!' I shouted, leaping up and down like a mad thing. 'Goal, goal, GOAL!'

The others were celebrating further up the pitch, but then Lauren ran right down to my goal to give me a big hug. We jumped up and down with our arms around each other, screaming with delight.

'Don't lose concentration, now,' Ria called anxiously. 'Focus!'

I pulled a face at Katy as we all took our positions for the kick-off.

'Doesn't that old dragon *ever* loosen up?' I muttered. 'Can't she see we're the better team here? She doesn't have to yell at us so much!'

'Going to tell her that at half-time, are you?' Katy asked, looking amused.

'I might!' I retorted. Even though I was enjoying the game enormously, Ria's constant yelling was annoying me no end. She was shouting so much that, like I'd said to Hannah, I couldn't get a word in at all – and I was on the pitch, for God's sake! I mean, it was my *duty* to yell at the others and let them know what was going on. After all, I was a goalie so I could see all the play unfolding in front of me. I honestly believed that *sometimes* the players on the pitch knew best, better than the coach, because they were right in the thick of it all. I didn't think that was a point of view that Ria would be very happy about, though!

The Foxes seemed quite dispirited by our goal, and they really didn't trouble us at all before half-time. I had nothing to do except take the odd goal kick, which was quite dull. The only shot the Foxes had was that free kick, and apart from that, I didn't have to make a single save. The Stars, on the other hand, were surging forward every chance we got, and Grace, Ruby and Hannah had all gone close to scoring several times.

When the ref blew for half-time, I hesitated for a moment as the others went to get a drink. Then I ran over to my dad, Luke and Jack.

'Come to see how football *should* be played, boys?' I said with a grin.

'Yep, absolutely,' Luke agreed. 'What do you reckon, Jack?'

'Yeah, I can see where I've been going wrong, now,' Jack replied thoughtfully. 'I need to tie some ribbons onto my footie boots.'

I turned bright red. 'Oh, that was just the other girls messing around,' I mumbled. Trust them to notice the ribbons before I'd had time to get rid of them!

'That was a first-class throw that set Lauren off for her goal,' Dad said, patting me on the back. 'Well done, love.'

'I threw the ball a bit too hard,' I said, but secretly I was delighted to see that Luke and Jack were both nodding in agreement with my dad. 'Lauren managed to keep it in play, though.'

'Georgie?' Ria was coming towards us. 'Off you go and join the others, please. I need to talk to you all before the second half.' She looked at my dad. 'Nice to see you again, Mr Taylor.'

'You too,' said Dad. 'Meet my sons, Luke and Jack.'

I stood aside a little grumpily as Ria shook hands with my brothers.

'Do you two play football?' asked Ria.

'For our school team,' Jack replied.

'Great stuff,' Ria said with a smile. *Oh, my God! I can't believe it! She actually smiled!* 'Football talent obviously runs in your family, because I hear that your brother is an apprentice at Melfield United.'

Luke nodded. 'It's just Georgie who's the odd

83

one out!' he said, grinning from ear to ear. 'Isn't it, Georgia?'

'Don't call me that,' I muttered, giving him a shove.

Ria laughed (*actually laughed!*). 'Nonsense. Georgie's very talented too!' she replied. I nearly fell over with shock. 'And I can see how proud your family are of you, Georgie,' Ria went on, turning to look at me. 'They were cheering and clapping like crazy when you set up that goal.'

I stared doubtfully at her. Was she winding me up? Could Luke and Jack *really* have been cheering me on?

'Well done, Georgie,' Ria continued. 'That was good vision on your part. Now, off you go and get a drink before the second half.'

I just about managed to stop my mouth from falling wide open in shock. What was Ria's game? Why was she being so nice all of a sudden? Maybe it was all part of her plan to get my dad on her side, so that I'd behave myself in future. But Ria had a long, long way to go before I'd like and respect her as much as I'd liked and respected Freya...

As I went across the pitch to join the others, I glanced back over my shoulder. Despite saying she wanted to talk to the team, Ria was still chatting to my dad, Luke and Jack, and my brothers seemed to be hanging on her every word. I could hardly believe it! I mean, they'd always been so rude about girls playing football, even if they *were* only teasing, but there they were having a good old gossip with Ria. OK, I admit it, I felt a *teeny* bit jealous.

Oh, all right then – I was REALLY GREEN WITH ENVY! And I was annoyed, too. My brothers knew I wasn't getting along that well with Ria, so why couldn't they stick by me and be on *my* side just once in a while?

'What's the matter, Georgie?' Jasmin thrust a bottle of water at me. 'Your face is down to your knees.'

'Yes, if you haven't noticed, we're winning one-nil,' Lauren pointed out, still glowing with triumph after her goal.

'It's Ria,' I muttered, taking a gulp of water. 'Why is she yelling at us so much? And—' I glanced suspiciously across the pitch to see Ria *still* talking to Luke and Jack. 'Why is she being so *nice* all of a sudden?'

Grace gave me an amused glance. 'Georgie, have you ever stopped to consider that Ria loves football as much as we do?' she asked. 'She's passionate about it – that's why she's yelling!'

I shrugged. 'Well, I bet there are rules about coaches shouting all the time,' I muttered.

'What about parents?' Hannah sighed, pulling a funny face. We all laughed. Mr Fleetwood, Hannah's dad, used to be a *terrible* shouter from the sidelines, so much so that he used to put Hannah right off her game. He's lots better now, but the occasional yelp still escapes him!

'Look, Ria will probably calm down a bit when she gets more experienced,' Katy offered. 'I mean, this *is* her first coaching job—'

'How do you know that?' I butted in.

'I overheard her talking to your dad in the car park on Thursday after training.' Katy tipped her bottle up and swallowed the last few drops. 'So she'll need time to settle in.'

'My dad was asking me how we were getting along with Ria,' Grace remarked. 'And when I told him how stern and strict she was, he said that he was *exactly* the same every time he started with a new class in September.' Grace's dad was a teacher at a boys' secondary school in Melfield. 'My dad said that it was better to start off strict and get the discipline sorted, then you could relax a bit later on.'

'Oh, please!' I scoffed. 'What are you lot making

all these excuses for? I still think Ria is just about the *worst* coach we could possibly—'

Suddenly Jasmin began hopping uncomfortably from one foot to the other. 'Sour-faced old dragon alert!' she muttered under her breath.

Ria had finally managed to tear herself away from my family and was coming over to us.

'I don't have much to say, girls,' she began with a smile (*another* one – she'd probably have to go and have a lie-down to recover, at this rate). 'You're doing very well, and you've got the Foxes on the run. One goal isn't much though, so we need to try and extend that lead in the second half. The main thing is to keep playing the way you have been, but make sure you stay steady and don't lose your heads. Push for a goal whenever you can, but don't take any foolish risks. Understood?'

We nodded as the ref indicated that the second half was about to start.

'Oh, she looks a lot less scary when she smiles!' Jasmin sighed with relief when we ran back onto the pitch. 'Maybe she's going to be an OK coach, after all.'

'We'll see,' I muttered, still feeling more than a touch grumpy.

The Foxes joined us on the pitch, looking rather glum. I'd noticed their manager giving them a pep talk at half-time, but it didn't seem to have made much difference to their morale. They were ours for the taking, I was sure of it.

We kicked off and almost scored in the first five minutes when Grace hit a screamer right towards the top corner of the Foxes' net. There was a gasp from the crowd but the ball didn't quite dip enough and it soared just over the crossbar.

'Look out!' I yelled, cupping my hands around my mouth as a Foxes defender raced to get the ball. 'I think they're going to take the goal kick quickly!'

'Watch out for the quick goal kick!' Ria roared at exactly the same moment. We looked at each other, and Ria raised her eyebrows at me, like I should keep quiet. Well! How loud and annoying was *she*? I scowled as I adjusted my gloves. I was pretty sure there must be rules about how coaches should conduct themselves on the pitch, and—

'GEORGIE!' There was a combined shriek from Hannah, Emily and Grace. 'LOOK OUT!'

I blinked. I'd been so busy thinking about Ria that I'd lost concentration slightly. Somehow, the Foxes' centre-forward had managed to get away from everyone else, and was zooming down the pitch towards me and my goal, the ball at her feet.

I made an instant decision and dashed straight out of my penalty area.

'Georgie!' I heard Ria shout. 'Get back! You don't need to come out—'

I ignored her. I was already out of my area, and it was just the Foxes' centre-forward and me. I wouldn't be able to use my hands to stop the ball, but I was confident I could tackle her and halt her in her tracks that way.

'Get back, Georgie!' called Katy, who was pounding up the field towards us. 'I can stop her!'

By the time I'd realised that Katy's pace would have saved us, it was too late. I was too far out of my area, and I was already committed to the tackle. Keeping my eye on the ball, I slid in to capture it and sweep it away. But somehow I MISSED. The centre-forward dummied me and was gone, heading towards my EMPTY goal, leaving me sat speechless on the grass.

I jumped up and collided heavily with Katy, who was racing past me. Meanwhile, the Foxes' centre-forward almost *walked* the ball jauntily into the net, and then turned to celebrate with her team-mates.

And that was how the match finished. 1-1.

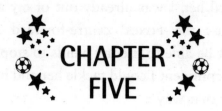

CHAPTER FIVE

The Fairmount Foxes celebrated the end of the game like they'd won promotion and the County Cup all rolled into one. They jumped in the air and whooped excitedly and exchanged high-fives. Meanwhile, the Stars walked off the pitch in gloomy silence, faces as long as wet weekends. I was so embarrassed, I pretended to fumble around in the back of my net for a few minutes, picking up the ribbons and my cap that I'd chucked in there earlier, just so that I didn't have to walk in with the others.

It was all my fault, I thought miserably. I'd made a fatal error in not realising that Katy was fast enough to catch up with the Foxes' centre-forward. I should have come a little way out of my goal to put her off, ready to fling myself at her feet if Katy *didn't* make it in time. And Katy had collided with me so quickly after I'd flunked the tackle, I knew that, between us, we might have prevented the goal.

If only I'd stayed put and not lost my head and dashed madly out of my area. The fact that I'd seen several Premiership goalies do exactly the same thing on TV was no consolation...

The Foxes had been so thrilled by the equaliser that they'd played like demons after that, determined to hold on and get a precious point. And they had.

I trudged across the field. I was the last to leave, apart from the Foxes' goalie. We shook hands, and then I headed towards the changing-room. There was no sign of Ria anywhere. Probably she was waiting somewhere, ready to leap out and tear me to shreds for ignoring her instructions.

I felt almost tearful as I pushed open the changing-room door. As I walked in, it felt like *everyone* in there, our team as well as the other Stars girls, turned to stare accusingly at me.

'Sorry, guys,' I muttered. 'That was down to me.'

'God, Georgie, so you made a mistake.' Grace was pulling her shirt over her head and her voice was muffled so I only just caught her next words. 'We've all been there and done that.'

'Haven't we just,' Jasmin said ruefully. 'It was *me* who tripped and lost the ball to the Foxes' girl just before she scored.'

'Oh, was it?' I said with a sigh. Typical Jasmin. She plays brilliantly for ages and then she inexplicably falls over her own feet.

'It's a bit of a downer, though, isn't it?' Lauren sighed. 'I really thought we were on for the three points there.'

'It would have been a great start to our promotion battle,' Hannah agreed.

I slumped down into the bench and put my head in my hands. 'Make me feel worse, why don't you?'

'Oh, come on, Georgie,' Katy said encouragingly. 'Yes, you let in a goal—'

'Ouch!' I groaned.

'But we had the chances to win three- or four-one,' Katy went on. 'I should really have got that header in from Lauren's corner.'

'I missed a few, too,' Grace confessed.

'And Ruby missed a virtually open goal,' Hannah

added. 'A five-year-old could have scored that one.'

'Hey! I heard that!' Ruby called indignantly from the loos.

'So it wasn't *all* your fault that we lost,' Katy finished.

'Bet Ria doesn't see it that way,' I said, pulling a face.

We were almost changed when the door opened. Ria looked in, and I felt quite sick as my stomach turned over.

'Girls, I'd like a very quick word with you all before you leave,' Ria said solemnly. 'Meet me outside as soon as you're ready.'

'This is it,' I sighed, when Ria had gone. 'She's going to rip me to pieces now.'

'Don't say that, Georgie,' Grace told me. 'We should *all* have done better today.'

'Yes, but I'm the one who let in the goal,' I pointed out.

It was a very glum, gloomy and sorrowful team who filed out of the changing-room to meet Ria outside on the pitch. I kept back, trying to stay out of sight behind Hannah and Grace, but then I noticed Ria staring at me so I moved forward defiantly. Let her do her worst!

'OK, so that wasn't exactly what we were hoping for today,' Ria began mildly enough. 'But the one thing I *don't* want is for you to get completely down about it. You're a good team – much better than the Foxes – and you should have won today. However, it's still the very beginning of the season, and we have plenty of time to get things right—'

At first I was glad that Ria was being quite nice and positive. But *that* didn't last long!

'You obviously need some intensive coaching in certain areas, and that's exactly what we're going to be focusing on. I feel that things have got a bit sloppy, in some ways, and you need more discipline to get the best out of yourselves.'

Whoa! Back up a bit there! Was Ria saying that Freya had been *sloppy*? That she was a better coach than Freya? My temper began to rise.

'Some of you obviously aren't used to *listening* and *obeying orders*, and that's something we're going to have to work on. It's important to keep in touch with your coach during a game.' Ria glanced at me, and I glared at her. 'We'll be doing some intensive shooting practice, too. You had at least six clear-cut scoring chances today, and yet you only converted one of them. I know that Grace scored a lot of goals last season, but we need to put even more of them away to secure promotion – and let in fewer goals at the other end, too, of course.' She stared hard at me again. 'The defence is taking too many foolish risks—'

'Maybe we'd play better if you stopped yelling at us!' Oops! I hadn't meant to say anything at all, but little devil Georgie had got the better of me...

Ria looked taken aback.

'It's really off-putting,' I went on crossly (I was just getting warmed-up here!). 'Freya never really shouted at us – and we beat the Fairmount Foxes *twice* last season! We've got the same team now, so what's the difference? *You are!*'

'Georgie!'

I stopped abruptly as I heard Dad's voice from behind me. He had come round the side of the college from the car park, and was standing there looking at me. *Very sternly.* I supposed he'd wondered where I was. Trust him to arrive at exactly that moment...

'Thank you for your input, Georgie,' Ria said coolly. Now it was *my* turn to be taken aback, because I'd thought she was going to rip my head off. But, of course, she wouldn't do that in front of my dad. 'But I'd appreciate it if you were a little more polite about it.'

I squirmed inwardly and my gaze fell.

'However, I know I shout too much, and it's something I intend to work on.' I looked up again to see that Ria was smiling, and the others were smiling back at her! *Why?* 'Now, off you go and forget about today. I want you all in a positive mood at training next week, and then I want to see you all totally up for the match against the Turnwood Tigers next Saturday.'

You won't believe this, but everyone broke into applause! They clapped! I nearly died of shock. Furiously I nudged Hannah, who was standing next to me.

'What's *that* for?' I whispered as Ria walked off.

'Well, I just thought Ria talked a lot of sense,' Hannah replied, a slightly defensive look on her face. 'She didn't blame any one of us in particular for the defeat.'

'And she apologised for shouting so much,' Lauren added.

'No, she didn't,' I retorted. 'She just said she was going to work on it, that's all.'

Lauren stuck her tongue out at me. 'Same difference.'

'Ria could have been much tougher on you and me, Georgie,' Jasmin pointed out. 'But she wasn't.'

'Only because my dad turned up,' I shot back. God, I was feeling confused and irritated and unsettled, and it was all Ria's fault. 'I'd better go. I can see from the look on Dad's face that I'm in big trouble.'

'Don't forget we're meeting in the mall tomorrow,' Grace called after me.

I nodded.

'I know that losing puts you in a bad mood, Georgia,' Dad said as I joined him (*oh no, full name – that's bad!*). 'But it doesn't mean you should be rude and obnoxious to *anyone* – and that includes your coach.'

'Sorry,' I mumbled as we went back to the car park.

'I know you didn't want Freya to leave,' Dad said a bit uncomfortably, 'but—'

'Oh, it's fine, Dad,' I broke in. 'Don't worry about it.'

Dad looked relieved then tried to hide it. He's very kind, really, but he doesn't much like getting into any kind of emotional discussion. I think it upsets him. I couldn't remember if he'd always been like that, or if he'd changed after Mum died.

Luke and Jack were already in the car. Oh no, I'd forgotten all about those two clowns... My heart plummeted as they leaned out of the windows, yelling at me as we got closer.

'Hey, Georgie, didn't you know that goalies are *supposed* to stay inside the penalty area?' Luke chortled.

'OK, guys,' I muttered, trying to rise above it, but feeling a little hurt just the same. 'I made a mistake, OK? I'll know better next time.'

'Goalies are also *supposed* to save the ball, not gift the striker an open goal!' Jack joined in. 'That girl practically *walked* the ball into the net. She even stopped to have a chat with her mum in the crowd on the way!'

'She did not!' I said indignantly, and Jack and Luke collapsed into hysterical laughter.

'Stop it, you two,' Dad warned. But when I climbed into the passenger seat, I could still hear my brothers sniggering behind me.

You messed up, Georgie, I told myself. But it wasn't all my fault. It was Ria's fault too...

Sunday 13th – 11am

Haven't got time to write much because I'm meeting the other girls at the mall. We'll hang out and have milkshakes at our favourite café Mamma Mia's and go shopping, and as usual, I won't buy anything except maybe a new hoodie or a pair of trainers, and the others will go mad over all the pink, sparkly, girlie stuff and buy loads! Actually, that's not quite true – Katy doesn't buy much usually, either. But she joins in when all the others are oohing and aahing over little miniskirts and pretty T-shirts and things like that. I just get bored and start pretending to yawn, which drives the other girls crazy!

Secretly, though, I'm dead confused, to be honest. There are so many shops, and so much choice, I can actually feel myself getting all hot and sweaty and panicky whenever we go into Topshop or Miss Selfridge or New Look. I haven't got a clue what suits me, and that's why I stick to trackies and hoodies and plain T-shirts – oh, and my Spurs shirt.

It's much easier that way. Boring, too, but I'd never admit that to anyone…

Oh no, now I'm late – still, it only takes me five minutes to get ready. Not like Lauren and Grace, they always look like they've stepped off a catwalk. It takes them about ten minutes just to put their make-up on after a match – I'm good to go in half the time!

Talking of footie, I bet we end up talking about Ria today at some point. I'm still gutted that we only managed a draw yesterday, especially as Luke and Jack haven't stopped teasing me about it since. But I've decided it wasn't all my fault – not really. Yep, I should have been concentrating, but Jasmin admitted it was *her* fault the Foxes' striker got clear.

God! That is *so* Jasmin! Don't get me wrong, I love her to bits – she's a great mate, and she's got this giggle that just makes *everybody* smile. But she can be so *daft* sometimes! She's a good midfielder and she scores the odd goal, but then suddenly she'll trip over her own feet or mistime a tackle or lose her head and do something stupid. I've lost count of the times the opposition have scored or *nearly* scored because of something Jasmin's done! But I guess all the good things she does on the pitch would cancel those out, anyway.

Now I really AM late! There's Mrs Sharma's car outside.

She's dropping me and Jasmin off at the mall...

'Georgie, give me your expert opinion.' Jasmin whisked two T-shirts – one pink, one green – off the chrome rack in front of us and held them up against her, one after the other. 'What do you think?'

I stared at her in amazement. 'What are you asking *me* for?'

'Because we've decided to educate you in the ways of girls,' Jasmin replied. 'It was Lauren's idea.'

'Jasmin, you've got a big mouth,' Lauren called. She and Grace were at a jewellery stand, trying on bracelets and earrings, while Hannah and Katy were browsing through the sale bins. 'It was supposed to be a *secret*.'

'Well, you shouldn't have told me, then,' Jasmin said cheerfully, putting both T-shirts back on the rack. 'You know I can't keep a secret to save my life.'

'So what's all this about then?' I asked. A flash of turquoise on a rail caught my eye as I half-turned to look at Lauren. It was a simple T-shirt dress, turquoise and white striped, and I wondered, very briefly, if it would suit me. But almost immediately I dismissed the idea. Jack and Luke would never let me live it down if I wore a *dress*! I had to be bribed with Spurs tickets to be a bridesmaid for my Aunt Danielle two years ago, and I've never lived down the hideous, frilly pink thing I had to wear.

'We're helping you discover your feminine side, Georgie,' Lauren explained. 'For instance—' She glanced swiftly around the rails, and then grabbed the striped T-shirt dress I'd just been looking at. She held it up against me. 'This would *really* suit you.'

'I don't wear dresses,' I said automatically. However, I did sneak a peek in the mirror. Lauren was perfectly right – the bright turquoise colour suited my lightly tanned skin and dark colouring.

'Try it on, Georgie,' Grace urged, but I shook my head.

Lauren sighed loudly and returned the dress to the rail. 'That's your trouble, Georgie,' she said. 'You never want to try *anything* new!'

I felt instantly on the defensive, but tried not to show it. 'What, you mean you don't love me just the way I am?' I joked.

'Oh, of *course* we do,' Jasmin chipped in. 'But trying new things is good, isn't it?'

'Some of the time, anyway,' Grace added, glancing at me with sympathy. I felt even more uncomfortable. I realised that Grace, who'd known me longer than any of the others, had guessed how I felt about things changing after my mum died. *Was* I stuck in a rut? *Was* I boring? I didn't know, but

I suspected I was. It was *safe* that way, though.

'There are some fab things in the sale bins!' Hannah rushed over to us, carrying a long string of black beads, and a crumpled white vest top, her face flushed with triumph. Katy followed her, holding a denim jacket decorated with zips and badges. 'Come and see.'

I was glad they'd interrupted us. But as we crossed the shop with them, Lauren sidled over to me.

'One day I'm going to get my hands on you and give you a make-over from top to toe, Georgia Taylor,' she warned.

'You'll have to catch me first,' I retorted, poking my tongue out at her and pretending to be annoyed. Secretly, though, I did think a makeover *might* be a good laugh. But it would only be for fun. I wasn't changing the way I looked for *anybody*.

'So what about the match yesterday?' Grace began. She took a black velvet beret from one of the sale bins and pulled it down over her blonde hair, where of course it looked instantly stylish. If I'd tried it, I would've looked like a French comedian! 'I thought Ria was pretty cool the way she handled everything.'

'So did I,' Hannah agreed, and the enthusiasm in her tone annoyed me. 'We *didn't* play our best, but she spoke to us afterwards as a team. She didn't single anyone out for criticism.'

'Like me, you mean,' I muttered.

'And me,' Jasmin added.

'I think she was OK,' Katy said, but she sounded a lot more cautious. 'I have to say, her shouting put me off, though.'

'And I thought she was well out of line when she criticised Freya,' I said.

'Did she?' Jasmin's eyes widened. 'I don't remember that bit.'

'Ria said we were sloppy and needed more discipline,' Lauren chimed in. 'Yeah, I thought that was a bit off, too.'

I felt better. So I *wasn't* the only one who didn't think Ria was oh-so-wonderful.

'OK, is it time for milkshakes now?' I asked. 'Because if I have to look at one more sparkly, shiny thing, I think I'll heave.'

'After that make-over, you'll change your mind,' Lauren promised. 'Mini-skirts, leggings, funky jewellery, kitten-heeled boots, hair and make-up – the real deal!'

'Ooh, is Georgie having a make-over?' Jasmin squealed with excitement.

'No, Georgie is *not* having a make-over,' I replied, leading them out of the shop.

'Actually, now I come to think of it, I don't have a spare couple of weeks, anyway,' Lauren said.

'You cheeky monkey!' I spluttered as the others collapsed into giggles.

A few moments later, as we made our way through the mall to Mamma Mia's, I spotted Luke standing by the glass lift that ran between the different floors.

'Look, it's my dumbo brother,' I said. 'I wonder if he's with his girlfriend, Lucy. Shall we go and wind him up?'

We all trooped over to him. Luke didn't look very pleased when he finally saw us.

'Oh, God, it's the invasion of the Purple Petunias,' he muttered, rolling his eyes.

'Been stood up, have we?' I asked sweetly.

'No, my girlfriend's buying something in Warehouse,' Luke retorted. Then he scowled, as if he thought he'd given too much away.

'Maybe we'd better wait and say hello to her,' I suggested naughtily. I had no intention of hanging around to meet yet another blonde birdbrain, but I knew it would annoy Luke no end. It did. He turned bright red.

'Just get out of here,' Luke snapped. He turned his back on us, and we all grinned.

We were just about to leave when a tiny, doll-like girl with long flowing blonde hair wearing a mini-skirt and red boots with spindly, skyscraper heels teetered towards us. I knew this just *had* to be Lucy!

'Luke?' she called, casting a curious glance at us.

Luke spun round so fast, he almost knocked Katy over.

'Sorry,' Luke muttered, leaping forward to grab Lucy's hand. 'C'mon, let's go.'

Well, it was my sisterly duty to introduce myself, wasn't it?

'Hi,' I said, stepping forward, 'I'm Luke's sister, Georgie. And you must be Lucy?'

The girl's face fell.

'No, actually my name's Chloe!' she snapped, looking rather peeved. Luke's face turned a bright, angry red as he glared at me.

'I finished with Lucy ages ago, Georgie!' he snarled.

'What?' I was genuinely taken aback. 'But you were going on about how gorgeous she was only last week—' I stopped abruptly. Chloe now looked like thunder, and she was staring sternly at Luke. He'd obviously told her a different story about him and Lucy. Meanwhile, Luke was still staring at *me*, and he had this *I'm going to kill you later* look on his face. I'd *really* gone and put my foot in it now, and I hadn't meant to...

I didn't dare glance at the other girls, but I knew they'd be busting their guts trying not to laugh. I was so flustered, I didn't know whether to just walk away or try to make things better.

'Er, these are my mates from football,' I gabbled, desperate to change the subject. 'We all play for the Springhill Stars.'

'Or the Purple Petunias, as I call them,' Luke scoffed.

'Don't you think girls should play football then?' Chloe asked him coolly.

'Well, they'll never be as good as the guys, will they?' Luke replied, looking relieved that Chloe was still talking to him.

'I think it's great that girls are doing things like playing football and rugby,' Chloe said, tossing back her long blonde locks. 'Why should boys have all the fun?'

We all stared at her with respect, except for Luke

who looked completely gobsmacked. Secretly, I was delighted that sweet little Chloe was showing some girl power – it might make Luke think twice about dissing the Stars!

'Have you ever done karate or kick-boxing, Luke?' Chloe went on. 'I have. I'm a karate black belt, by the way. I could pin you down on the floor right now, and you wouldn't be able to do a thing about it. Even though you're a *guy*.'

'Er, we'd better be going,' I said quickly, as Luke fixed me with the evil eye. 'Nice to meet you, Lu— I mean, Chloe!' It wasn't deliberate, I *swear*.

The six of us rushed off. We just made it around the next corner before we howled with laughter.

'Did you see Luke's face when you called her Lucy?' Lauren gasped. 'It was a classic!'

'And when she asked him if he did karate or kick-boxing,' Grace added. 'She was so annoyed, I thought she was going to floor him with one kick, there and then!'

I was laughing just as hard as the others, but secretly I couldn't help feeling a bit worried. I hadn't meant to embarrass Luke like that – and I'd seen the look he gave me as we walked away.

Now all I had to do was wait and see how

he'd get his own back. Because I knew he would, somehow...

Sunday 13th - 3.45pm

Home now, and just writing this before I go downstairs to watch the Big Match, Arsenal vs Liverpool. God, my feet are killing me after all that shopping, and I was wearing trainers! I honestly don't know how Chloe walked around the shopping mall in those high heels – I would have tripped over a million times.

Talking of Chloe, Luke's really mad at me about what happened at the mall. When I got home, he was waiting to have a row with me – so, of course I had to join in, didn't I! I feel a bit mean now, because I should have said sorry for mixing Chloe and Lucy up, but how was I to know he'd changed girlfriends so recently? I'm not a mind-reader! Anyway, he didn't give me a chance to say sorry because he tore right into me, so I had to stand up for myself. That's what it's like in this house...

Oh, well, apart from the whole Luke-Chloe-Lucy thing, and my poor aching feet, I had a great time as usual with the girls. Grace was a bit down again when we first met up, although she didn't say why. I wonder *if her parents have been rowing again. She cheered up when we started shopping, though.*

You know, it's amazing how much money Lauren has! She spent a fortune, more than all the others put together, and it was mostly on rubbish, too. Her parents must have more money than sense! She kept going on about giving me a make-over all the time we were in Mamma Mia's, but she was teasing – I hope! I don't want to look like Lauren, all glossy and girlie and polished and pink and pouty. I just want to be ME!

Suddenly the bedroom door flew open. I wasn't expecting it and I almost fell off my bed with shock. I shoved my diary quickly under the duvet as Luke stuck his head in.

'Dad sent me to tell you the match is starting,' he said, shooting me a nasty glare. 'And he said if we argue while it's on, we're in trouble.'

'OK,' I muttered.

I waited until Luke had gone downstairs again, banging the door behind him. Then I retrieved my diary from under the duvet. No one in my family knew I had a secret diary, not even Adey, and I talked to him more than anyone else. I can say anything

I like in my diary, and it is kind of almost like an extra friend (if that doesn't sound just too sad!).

I shoved the little red book back in its usual hiding-place, the wicker laundry basket where I put my dirty clothes, ready for washing. No one ever looked in there – we did our own washing in this house!

Luke and I were at each other's throats again, and Ria and I weren't getting along any better. I sighed. I had a doomy, gloomy feeling in the very pit of my stomach, and I couldn't help worrying about what lay ahead...

CHAPTER SIX

Tuesday 15th – 5.45pm

I got a lunchtime detention today from Miss Burton during maths. My mate Sushila was asking me how I was getting on with Ria (because I'd had a big old moan to her last week) when Miss Burton told us off for talking and gave us detention. God, I hate school sometimes!

When I got home from school, Adey was here and we had a drink and a chat. He'd tried to make banana muffins from one of Mum's recipes, but he'd forgotten to put the baking powder in and they didn't rise! They tasted OK, though.

Adey asked me, like Sushila had, how I was getting on with Ria. I shrugged and said it wasn't just me, that the others didn't like her much either. OK, maybe that was stretching the truth a *teensy weensy* bit – but Katy and Lauren are on my side, and Jasmin keeps insisting that she's scared of her, so I wasn't far wrong! Adey started going on yet again about how I had to make a choice between the good of the team and my own feelings. I didn't know what to say to that, but luckily Jack and Luke turned up from school just then and began teasing Adey about his flat muffins, so that was that.

I guess what I would have said was that Ria isn't just annoying me, I don't think she's any good for the team either...

Now I'm late again! Must get ready for training.

'OK, I need to have a quick word with you all before we start,' Ria announced as we came out of the changing-room onto the pitch.

I glanced over at Dad, who was sitting on a nearby bench. Sometimes he went home and came back for me, sometimes he stayed in the car and sometimes he went to the college cafeteria, but occasionally, like some of the other parents, he stayed to watch the training session. Grace's dad, Mr Kennedy, was sitting next to him.

'It's about the Open Day at the Melfield United ground,' Ria went on. 'It's only a week and a half away, now.'

My ears pricked up immediately. I thought Ria had forgotten all about the Open Day.

'I've suggested to the other coaches that we team up with the Melfield United girls' teams to organise some short exhibition matches,' Ria told us. 'Some of you may already be committed to other things that particular Sunday afternoon, but we'd like as many of you as possible to turn up. The fair is raising money for the local hospice, but it's also a great chance to show off our club and maybe recruit some new players.' She swung round and targeted me. 'Georgie?'

'Er, yes?' I stammered, taken completely by surprise.

'I thought it would be good if some of the goalies ran a sideshow where children could take shots and try to score against them.' Ria looked enquiringly at me. 'Would you be up for that?'

'Well – um – OK,' I mumbled, although I was secretly delighted to be asked.

'Don't worry,' Ria said. 'The children will all be

under five years old, but I'm sure you'll save a few if you play to your best.'

I stared at her in disbelief. '*What*?' I spluttered, my face creasing into a ferocious frown.

'Milkshake, Georgie!' Hannah said in my ear. Milkshake is this secret word we use when we think one of us is going to lose it – and believe me, I was on the edge right then!

'That was a joke, Georgie,' Ria explained patiently. The others burst into giggles – including my mates, the traitors! 'We thought about restricting it to the under-tens, if you're OK with that?'

I nodded. I was glad that Ria was organising us to take part in the Open Day, but I felt a bit upset about it, too. *Freya* should be doing all this – after all, she'd actually known and liked my mum. Ria hadn't, so she probably wasn't interested in supporting the hospice at all. Perhaps she just wanted to try and get some new players for the team, or maybe she just enjoyed bossing everybody about!

Unfortunately, I made the mistake of saying all this aloud to Lauren as we were passing in pairs, moving up and down the pitch.

'That's a bit unfair, Georgie,' Lauren replied with a frown. 'I bet Ria wants to help the hospice, too.'

'Why are *you* standing up for Ria?' I asked in amazement, sliding a pass neatly into Lauren's path. 'I thought you didn't like her.'

'I never said that, Georgie!' Lauren shook her head. 'We're still getting to know her.'

'So?' I glanced over at Ria. 'She's never going to be like Freya, is she?'

'No, but she might still be a great coach,' Lauren said annoyingly.

'Too hard, Grace!' Ria called as Grace, who was Jasmin's partner, over-hit the ball. It went spinning away from Jasmin, but she managed to lunge forward and capture it, killing the bounce stone-dead.

To my surprise, Ria applauded. 'Well done, Jasmin,' she said. 'That was brilliant.'

'And I didn't trip over my own feet – yay, me!' Jasmin said, throwing her arms into the air in a victory salute.

'There's still time,' Ria said drily. Jasmin stared at her, eyes wide, and then began to laugh. Ria grinned at her, too.

Was it me, or was there something *weird* going on around here? Everyone was being far too nice to Ria for my liking...

I was happily minding my own business, joining

in with dribbling around coloured cones, when Ria beckoned me out of line.

'Come with me, Georgie,' she said, leading me over to a set of goalposts. The keepers from the Under-Eleven, Under-Twelve and Under-Fourteen teams were already waiting there. 'Mac's going to keep an eye on the others while we do some intensive goalie training.' Danny Macdonald was the coach of the Under-Twelves team.

'But I like practising with the rest of my team,' I muttered.

'Yes, and it's important that you improve your outfield skills, of course,' Ria agreed smoothly. 'A goalie's all-round skills are much more important these days because of changes to the back pass rule. Now you have to be able to take a quick, accurate kick under pressure from the opposition. You may even be forced to head the ball away if a back pass from a team-mate goes wrong! But—' Ria locked gazes with me. 'It's also important for us to practise *specific* goalkeeping skills. Georgie, you can partner Alannah. Madison, you team up with Lalita.'

I moved over to stand next to Alannah, who was the Under-Twelve team's goalie.

'Bossy, isn't she?' I complained under my breath.

Alannah looked at me in amazement. 'She's a coach – they're supposed to tell us what to do!' she said with a shrug. 'Anyway, Ria used to be a goalie herself, so she knows what she's talking about.'

'*Ria* was a goalie?' I exclaimed, surprised.

Alannah nodded. 'Yep.' She threw Ria an admiring glance. 'I think she's *cool*.'

I was silent. I was beginning to feel quite isolated and I didn't like it. But I didn't have much time to think about it for the next twenty-five minutes. Ria had us doing all sorts. We had to practise throwing the ball at each other's head, shoulders and stomachs so that we could save it. Then we practised diving and falling to the side, scooping the ball up off the ground and also passing it through each other's legs. Then we had a tug of war in pairs, with one keeper trying to get the ball off the other.

'Oh *bum*!' I groaned, as Alannah finally managed to wrestle the ball away from me.

Ria shook her finger at me. 'Milkshake, Georgie!' she said.

My mouth fell open as I stood and stared at her.

'Stop catching flies, Georgie, and let's finish with some shooting,' Ria went on briskly. 'Take it in turns to go in goal, and the other three get five shots each.'

By the time we'd all done a stint in goal, the session was over.

'You looked like you were having fun, Georgie,' Jasmin said, slinging her arm around my shoulders as we trooped off the field.

'Well, it was OK,' I admitted reluctantly. 'I'd rather be with you guys, though.' Then I frowned. 'This is crazy, but did someone tell Ria about the milkshake thing?'

'Oh, that was me,' Hannah admitted without a trace of embarrassment.

'Why?' I demanded as we went into the changing-room.

'Well, Ria heard me saying it to you earlier, and she asked me what it meant, so...' Hannah's voice trailed away as she realised I was glaring at her. 'Is there a problem?'

'I just don't think we should be telling her that kind of stuff,' I complained, although I knew it wouldn't have bothered me one bit if Hannah had told *Freya* instead.

'Oh, chill out, Georgie,' Lauren chimed in as we trooped into the changing-room. 'I mean, it's just a *word*. It's not like we made it up or anything.'

'And Ria thought it was funny when I told her

how we chose the word *milkshake*,' Hannah added. As if that was going to make me feel better!

'I'm starting to like Ria,' Katy confessed as she pulled off her shirt. 'She's really good at explaining stuff. She makes you see how we can use the tactics we practise at training in a real match.'

'Freya used to do that, too,' I butted in quickly. 'And to be honest, I *still* don't rate Ria. She's loud, she talks too much, she's too bossy and too opinionated—'

'She's also very passionate about football, she cares about getting things right, she's determined and stubborn, but I think she has a great sense of humour.' Katy gazed at me with a twinkle in her eyes. 'Remind you of anyone?'

For the second time that evening my mouth dropped open.

'You don't mean…? You don't think—?'

The others were laughing.

'Ria and I are nothing like each other!' I snapped, shoving my kit into my bag. Then I stomped out of the changing-room.

'Georgie!' Katy was calling after me. 'It was just a joke!'

I didn't turn back. I ran through the college and

out into the front car park, where Ria was standing talking to my dad and Mr Kennedy. I was really annoyed, although I knew that Katy was only winding me up. I didn't understand why I was taking it so seriously though – I mean, there was no truth in it at all!

And even if all the other girls had given in and gone over to Ria's side, she still hadn't done enough yet to impress *me*...

Tuesday 15th – 9pm

I just got a text from Katy saying she was sorry she'd upset me. So I sent a jokey reply saying she was never to compare me with Ria again, or I'd tie her to a tree with her own football boot laces and throw milkshakes at her, ha ha. Katy sent back another text, saying maybe we should have a chat about Ria, but I haven't answered it yet. And I'm not going to. I know that Katy is just *dying* to persuade me that Ria's turning out to be OK, and that I should just get on with it. But I don't have to like Ria just because all the other girls do...

That's Katy for you, though. She's a bit like Grace in that way. She thinks she's dead mature and grown-up about things, but I don't like ANYONE telling me what to do. I can make up my own mind about Ria, without Katy sticking her nose in, thank you very much! Anyway, Katy doesn't like it when the rest of us try to find out stuff about her home life – she just comes over all quiet and mysterious and moody. It drives me nuts! Like when we went to the mall last Sunday, she had to leave early but didn't say why...

And what about Hannah giving away our milkshake thing to Ria? I was pretty annoyed about that. Hasn't Hannah got any loyalty to us lot? I love Hannah to bits, but she's been a bit of a traitor, really. I never thought she had such a big mouth!

I just KNOW I'm going to get the Big Lecture about Ria and getting along and the good of the team and change is fantastic, *blah blah* and more *blah* for the rest of the week. I bet that Katy, Hannah and Grace will be giving me earache tomorrow at school, and Jasmin and Lauren will join in at training on Thursday night...

As it turned out, training on Thursday was actually OK. Ria did another goalies' session, and all right, I admit it – we did some useful stuff. End of. I'm not about to roll over and give in and become all friendly, just because she knows a lot about being a goalie...

To my surprise, though, Grace, Jasmin and the others had hardly hassled me at all about trying to sort out my relationship with Ria. But I'd noticed them giving each other meaningful, sideways glances and nods at training, so I wondered if maybe they were cooking up some kind of secret plan to force me and Ria to get along. They'd have to catch me first, though!

'Dad?' I tapped on the bathroom door. It was Friday night and I was about to head out to the park to meet the girls for our usual pre-match get-together. 'I'm off now.'

'Have a good time, love,' Dad called. 'And be back by seven-thirty.'

I wanted to tell him to have a good time, too, but I knew he was going out on a date, so somehow I couldn't quite force the words out. I knew, in my head, that Mum had been dead for three and a half years now, and that Dad had to have a life – Adey and I had talked about it before. But in my heart, it still felt too soon. We'd only met a couple of the five or six women Dad had dated so far, and nothing had ever got very serious, which was the way I liked it. Luke and Jack weren't very happy either whenever they knew Dad had a date. It was probably the only thing the three of us ever agreed on...

I grabbed my thick grey fleece because the nights were getting colder as autumn came closer, and then I clattered downstairs.

'Off to meet the Purple Petunias?' Luke called as I passed the open living-room door.

I stopped.

'You going to meet Chloe, or has she finished with you because of your old-fashioned views about women and sport?' I asked.

Luke scowled, so I figured I'd hit the nail *right* on the head.

'Jack and me'll be there at the Petunias' away game tomorrow, cheering you on,' he yelled after me as I swung open the front door. 'Better warn your mates.'

I groaned quietly to myself. I'd been hoping that now Luke and Jack had had their bit of fun, they'd get bored with coming to my matches. But anyway, I was *determined* that I wouldn't make any silly mistakes this time. I'd keep my head and save everything. No pressure, then!

When I got to the park, the other girls were all squashed onto 'our' bench reading the same magazine and passing it back and forth between them. Chelsea, Lauren's dog, was slumped at her feet, but she jumped up and waddled over to me for a stroke.

'What's the mag?' I asked idly, scratching Chelsea's ears.

'*Glam Girl*,' Lauren replied, flipping to one of the middle pages and handing the magazine to me. 'Look, they've done a fab makeover on this *totally* plain girl. Doesn't she look great?'

'And your point is?' I said, thrusting the magazine rudely back at her without looking at it.

'Anyone can look better with the right clothes, make-up and hairstyle.' Lauren stared up at me, a cheeky smile on her face. 'So there's hope for everyone – even you!'

'You're living very dangerously, Lauren Bell,' I warned in a mock-threatening tone. But as Lauren folded the magazine up and popped it into her bag, I caught a glimpse of the article. The girl *did* look amazing – from plain and ordinary to pretty and polished. I felt a stab of envy that I quickly pushed aside. I could *never* look like that.

'Shall we walk around for a bit?' Grace remarked. 'I think Chelsea's getting restless.'

We all glanced down to see Chelsea chewing on the toy monkey charm that hung off Jasmin's bag. Jasmin gave a shriek and leapt off the bench to retrieve it from Chelsea's teeth.

'So what about tomorrow's match, then?' said Hannah as we strolled through the park. 'We really need those three points after last week's disaster, don't we?'

'The Tigers are a better team than the Foxes,' Jasmin commented with a sigh. 'We need to be on top of our game, guys.'

'We're going to win tomorrow,' Katy predicted confidently. 'I think we'll play much better now that we've got to know Ria a little more—'

'Oh come on, if we *do* win, I doubt if Ria'll have anything to do with it,' I retorted. 'It'll be down to us, not her.'

We were nearing one of the park gates by now. As we passed by and continued to walk towards the playground, I just happened to glance out of the gates at the road which circled the park.

At that very moment an old black car drove past.

That looks like my dad's car, I thought.

The car slowed down for a red traffic light, and I saw that it *was* my dad's car.

He was driving, and sitting next to him in the passenger seat was Ria.

CHAPTER SEVEN

A split second later, the car accelerated away. The other girls walked on, still chattering and laughing.

But I just stood there. I couldn't move because I was numb all over. *My dad had said he had a date tonight. And I'd just seen him with Ria.*

I can't even remember what I was thinking. I was in shock. Ria – and my dad!

'Georgie?'

I heard a voice coming from miles away. I blinked and saw that Hannah was hurrying back towards me. The other girls were quite a way ahead, but they were looking round curiously.

'What's the matter, Georgie?' Hannah asked with her trademark wide, friendly grin. 'You look like you've seen a ghost!' But her smile gradually faded as she stared more closely at the expression on my face.

'Not a ghost.' I just about managed to get the words out. Looking concerned, the others were now rushing back towards us. 'Ria. With my dad.'

The look on Hannah's face would have been comical, if I hadn't been so upset. She gazed at me blankly until suddenly she understood what I was getting at.

'You mean—' Hannah stared at me, wide-eyed. 'Are you sure?' She turned to the others. 'Georgie just saw Ria with her dad!' Hannah blurted out.

'So?' Jasmin looked puzzled, and the others didn't seem to get it, either.

'Well, maybe they met each other by chance,' Lauren began.

'No!' Now that the first shock of discovery was over, I was starting to feel different emotions – anger and misery were flooding through me. 'Dad said he had a date tonight, but he didn't say who with. It's Ria. I've just seen them together in Dad's car.' My voice cracked a little, and I bit my lip.

There was a tense silence for a moment. None of the girls seemed to know what to say, even Grace who was usually quick to offer advice.

'Well, it doesn't actually *mean* anything, Georgie,' Lauren said hesitantly. 'Lots of people go on dates, it doesn't mean—' She stopped, looking awkward.

'Maybe they're just friends,' Jasmin suggested.

I shook my head. As my emotions began to spill over, I knew I had to get away.

'I'm going,' I muttered through clenched teeth. 'See you tomorrow.'

And then I ran.

'Georgie, wait!' I heard Grace yell.

I didn't stop. I speeded up, in fact. My head was spinning so much I felt sick, as I pounded through the streets back towards our house. *See you tomorrow*, I'd said. But would I actually be going to the game against the Turnwood Tigers after all? How could I? I'd have to face Ria, the traitor... Spending all that time chatting to my dad whenever she could. I'd thought they were talking about *me*, when really they just fancied each other! I felt sick. And Dad – he knew how I felt about Ria. How could he do this to me?

I let myself into the house really quietly because

I was still upset and I didn't want to bump into Luke and Jack. But luckily they were out. Adey was at the computer in the dining room, checking out his Facebook page, but he glanced round when I burst in.

'What's up?' he asked after one look at my face.

'Dad's out on a date with Ria!' I gasped.

Adey only looked mildly surprised, which annoyed me.

'O-K,' he said slowly. 'I take it you're not happy about it?'

'*Happy*?' I shrieked, my anger and hurt boiling up and spilling over. 'Too right I'm not happy – I can't stand her!'

'Chill out, Georgie.' Adey got up from the table and came over to me, but I pushed him away irritably. 'So Dad's gone for a drink with Ria. So what? It's hardly the crime of the century.'

'But – Dad knows I don't like her,' I stammered. 'I don't *want* him to go out with her!'

'Look, you *know* this isn't the first time that Dad's been out on a date since Mum died,' Adey pointed out gently. 'Try to understand, Georgie. I don't like it much, either, but he's lonely and he misses Mum—'

'Yes, but why does it have to be *Ria*?' I wailed. I didn't like to think about Dad being lonely. It made me feel so selfish. But I just *couldn't* stop myself from wishing that he wouldn't date *anyone*, not just Ria…

'Well, they might have just met up to talk about how you and she could get along better, who knows?' Adey pointed out. I was reluctant to admit it, but that *did* sound reasonably sensible. 'And even if they *do* like each other, what are you so scared of, Georgie?'

I struggled to understand my emotions. What *was* I scared of? That Dad and Ria would fall madly in love and get married and I'd have a wicked stepmother? They'd only met last week, and this was their first date, for God's sake, as far as I knew. There might not even be another. But Ria pushed all my buttons, and little devil Georgie was in overdrive.

'Dad should have told me,' I said stubbornly.

'Yep, maybe he should,' Adey agreed. 'You know what Dad's like, though – he's not good at dealing with emotional stuff. But he'll take things very slowly, Georgie. He won't rush into anything. And anyway, he wouldn't have wanted to upset you.

He knows how you feel about Ria.'

'So *why* did he ask her out then?' I demanded.

Adey sighed. 'Well, I don't know for sure, but I guess he thinks that things between you and Ria will settle down in a week or two, and that you're only reacting like this because you were so shocked when Freya left right out of the blue—'

'That's not true!' I broke in quickly, pushing aside the secret doubt that perhaps it *was* true. Just a little.

'I'm just telling you what Dad's probably thinking,' Adey said, giving me a sympathetic hug.

I nodded. Suddenly I felt exhausted and like I couldn't stand up for a minute longer.

'I'm going upstairs, Adey.'

'All right.' My brother looked at me with concern. 'I'll be here if you need to talk.'

I trailed upstairs and curled up on top of my bed. I wanted to cry and cry, but I wouldn't give Ria the satisfaction. For some reason Mum and Rainbow kept coming into my head, and it was hard to push those upsetting thoughts away.

Tired, emotional and stressed to the max, I must have somehow fallen asleep, lying on the bed in all my clothes, because a tap on my door jerked me awake.

'Uh – yeah?' I mumbled, sitting up and glancing at the clock. It was almost ten – I'd been flat out asleep for almost three hours.

Dad poked his head round the door. He looked supremely embarrassed, and I knew straightaway that he'd been talking to Adey. I felt myself flush too, from head to toe.

'All right, sweetie?' Dad came into my room. He cleared his throat, looking a bit like a naughty schoolboy who's been caught out. 'Adey said you saw me out with Ria...'

'Yes.' I dropped my eyes. My face was burning red, although I don't know why I felt so awkward. *I'd* done nothing wrong, after all.

Dad sighed. 'I didn't want you to find out like this, sweetheart. I *knew* I shouldn't have taken that short cut around the park...'

I stayed silent.

'We were just going for a drink, Georgie,' Dad explained. 'Nothing heavy or serious. I – um—' He cleared his throat again, loudly. 'Look, this is what happened. I met Ria in town earlier this week, by chance, during my lunch hour from work. We went for a quick coffee to talk about you because Ria was concerned you and she weren't getting along. Then we decided to meet up for a drink tonight. I know I should have mentioned it, and Ria did ask me to tell you, but I didn't get around to it...'

That was typical Dad. He hated arguments and confrontations and always tried to avoid them if he could. And I knew he would have done anything rather than hurt me. He was so soft-hearted, that's why I loved him. But right now I felt *betrayed*.

'So when were you going to tell me, Dad?' I burst out.

'Well, I didn't think there was any point if it was just the one date,' Dad murmured.

'And is it?' I demanded. 'Is it just the one date or not?'

Dad's face told its own story. I felt tears prickling my eyelids and I blinked fiercely.

'Georgie, you and the boys are more important to me than anything,' Dad said soberly. 'You'll always be my number one girl. But I can't sit around the house on my own forever—'

'I know, I know,' I sighed. Like I said, Adey and I had talked about this almost *every* time Dad had been out on a date for the last eighteen months. I'd argued that Dad wasn't alone, that he had Adey, Luke, Jack and me to come home to. But Adey

135

had made me realise that Dad was looking ahead to the future, to the time when we all grew up and left home. I'd tried *so* hard to understand and to be grown-up about it. But it was a long, hard struggle...

'Ria's a bit worried about you, love,' Dad went on. 'She told me she feels like she's getting to know all the other girls, but not you, yet.'

'Oh,' I mumbled. I had so much I wanted to say, but I knew I'd blurt out something I'd regret once I got started.

'Look, love, it makes sense for you to try and get along with Ria.' Dad was pacing nervously up and down my bedroom now, probably so that he didn't have to look me in the eye. 'Believe me, she's not going anywhere because she's very excited about this job. So, unless you want to change teams...' His voice trailed away.

'I'll be fine, Dad. Don't worry.' It cost me a huge effort to get the words out. I was hurting so much inside, I felt physically sick.

Dad didn't look very convinced but he dropped a quick kiss on top of my head and went out. I wanted to yell after him: *Dad, don't go out with Ria again!* But I knew I couldn't. Somehow, though,

I had to make them both realise that I wasn't putting up with this situation. *No way.* And because I didn't want to hurt Dad or fall out with him, I would have to make sure that it was Ria who got the message, loud and clear…

'OK, girls, we've got five minutes before the game starts.' Ria glanced at her watch. 'So gather round, and let's make sure we're all in the right frame of mind for today's match.'

She stared at me and I looked away as if I wasn't interested. My heart was thumping so loudly, I could hear it in my ears. We were standing outside on the pitch at Turnwood Sixth Form College, the sun was peeping out from behind puffs of white clouds and there was a slight, cooling breeze. An absolutely *perfect* day for football. My whole family were there to watch. Even Adey had come because he wasn't playing for Melfield United reserves today as he had a slight hamstring problem. I loved it when Adey was there to cheer me on. He took me and my football seriously, not like Luke and Jack. Dad had warned those two idiots to be on their best behaviour today and not to wind me up *too* much. So everything should have been perfect.

But I wasn't looking forward to the match today one bit.

'Are you OK, Georgie?' Lauren whispered anxiously in my ear.

I nodded, not looking at her. We'd arrived late because of the traffic, and the other girls were already changed and ready to go when I got there. They were going to hang around waiting for me, but Ria had herded them outside to warm up. I was secretly glad of it. I knew that Grace, Katy and the others were going to quiz me about what was happening with Ria and Dad. And I didn't want to talk about it, not even to them. I knew they'd tell me to try and make the best of it and get along with Ria and – YAWN. I'd heard it all before.

'Georgie?' Ria had been talking, but I wasn't listening. The sound of my name jerked me out of my thoughts, and I almost said *Yes?* Until I remembered what I'd decided.

'The Tigers have two very tall players,' Ria went on, glancing across at the opposition. 'They could be good with their heads, so watch out for high crosses. Katy and the rest of the defence will help you deal with them, OK?'

I gave a tiny shrug and remained silent. Ria

looked a bit taken aback. All right, all right, I know it's rude to ignore someone who's speaking to you, but how else could I show Ria exactly how hurt and angry and frustrated I was?

Katy, Jasmin and the others were all shooting sideways glances at me, but I ignored them, too. For a moment I thought Ria was going to tell me off, but she didn't. The referee was calling us onto the pitch now, and Ria smiled at us.

'Go for it, girls. I know you can get these three points.'

'Thanks, Ria!' everyone chorused. Except me. I'd turned abruptly and was walking over to my goalmouth before Ria had even finished speaking.

'Georgie!' Katy chased after me. 'What's going on?'

'Nothing,' I retorted. I glanced over my shoulder, and saw Ria standing on the touchline, staring back at me. The look on her face was unreadable.

'Don't give us that old rubbish.' Hannah ran to join us. 'You're ignoring Ria, aren't you, Georgie?'

'So what if I am?' I demanded. 'Do you expect me to be her best friend after last night?'

'No, but this isn't just about you and Ria, Georgie,' Grace had now come up behind us. She sounded quite stern, which was unlike her. 'This is about the *team*, too. We're not going to be playing our best if you and Ria are at each other's throats.'

'Thanks for the advice, Grace,' I said as coolly as I could, 'but I'm not going to let Ria affect my game.'

Hmm, told you I had a big mouth, didn't I? From the moment the Tigers won the toss and kicked off, I knew that Grace was right. I was edgy and nervous and I had to keep telling myself to *concentrate*. I couldn't help glancing across at Ria and Dad. She was standing quite near to him in the crowd, and my eyes kept straying across to them suspiciously every few minutes. I don't know why, they were hardly likely to start snogging on the touchline in front of everyone, were they?

I could also see Luke and Jack shooting suspicious, sideways glances at her every so often. Dad had told them this morning when we were getting breakfast that he'd been out with Ria last night. They'd both looked shocked, which cheered me up. I was hoping that, for once, we'd be on the same side, and that together we could talk Dad out of seeing Ria again.

'Bet you're thrilled about *that*, Georgie,' Luke had remarked, pouring himself a huge bowl of Cheerios.

I'd waited a few seconds until Dad had gone out of the kitchen before I replied.

'Yeah, I'm jumping up and down with joy, obviously,' I said.

'I can see why Dad asked her out, though,' Jack said thoughtfully. 'I mean, she's *hot*!'

'She is not!' I snapped.

'She so *is*,' Luke agreed, picking a stray Cheerio off the worktop and chucking it at me. 'And she knows all about football, too – the perfect woman!'

I'd stomped out of the kitchen in a temper, then. I *knew* they were just saying these things to annoy me. And I knew that Luke, in particular, was still mad because he blamed me for the split with Chloe, but then he was *always* mad at me for something or other. I was sure, though, that, like me, Luke and Jack didn't really want Dad to date *anyone*.

I turned slightly to gaze at Ria. She seemed to be trying her hardest not to yell at us today, although she was doing a lot of face-pulling and pointing and hand gestures, as well as rolling her eyes and pacing up and down. It was quite funny, actually. Well, it would have been if I didn't dislike her so much. I hoped my dad was watching her – some of those faces she was pulling would put anybody off.

Luckily, the Stars went ahead quite early in the first half, which gave me a slight breathing space and time to settle in. It was a brilliant move, starting with Hannah winning the ball after a Tigers' throw-in. She chipped it into the penalty area, and Grace was waiting to side-foot it into the net.

'Great stuff, guys!' I yelled at the top of my voice, cupping my hands around my mouth. The heat was off a little, but I hadn't forgotten what had happened against the Foxes when I took my eye off the ball for just a few seconds.

Katy gave me a double thumbs-up as she ran back into position for kick-off.

'Ria's not shouting much this game, is she?' she remarked with a grin. 'We must be doing something right!'

For a while after the goal, it was all the Stars. I didn't really have that much to do, which unfortunately left me too much time to keep staring over at Dad and Ria. Near the end of the first half, I saw her turn to say something to my dad, and he smiled. *What were they talking about?*

'Georgie!' That was Katy calling my name.

I glanced up the field and saw the Tigers' midfield heading towards my goal in a long line. In the centre was one of their tall strikers, the ball at her feet. She passed it to her left to a red-headed girl, and Emily tried to intercept but missed. The redhead completed the old one-two, and the striker came zooming straight into my penalty area. Katy was heading towards her on one side and Jo-Jo on the other, so although the striker was only just inside the area, she let one fly.

The shot was a beauty. Hard, high, fast and on target. I made an instant decision and flung myself across the goal towards the ball. It just hit the very tips of my fingers, but that was enough to deflect it from its journey into the net. The ball flew around the other side of the post and bounced harmlessly out of play.

There was a round of applause from the crowd and from the rest of the Stars, and I couldn't help blushing.

'Fantastic save, Georgie!' Jasmin gasped, belting half the length of the pitch to throw her arms around me.

'Way to go, Georgie,' said Debs, slapping me on the back as we hastily took our places for the Tigers' corner.

I couldn't resist glancing over at Ria. She smiled

and nodded at me and mouthed *Well done!* I was half-tempted to smile back, but I forced myself not to. It wasn't difficult, especially when I saw Dad tap her shoulder and say something in her ear. My heart sunk down into my boots, and I heaved a silent sigh. I felt as if my whole world was changing, and nobody cared, except me.

Why did Freya have to leave, I asked myself for the millionth time. If only things had stayed the same, I wouldn't be in this mess right now...

'Three-one! Three-one! Three-one!' Jasmin chanted at the end of the match. She zoomed around the grass with her arms held out like an aeroplane. 'And I scored one of them. Yay, me!'

'And me! I got one too!' Hannah grabbed Jasmin's arms and they tangoed half the length of the pitch like a couple on *Strictly Come Dancing*.

'They were all fab goals,' Lauren said, as we bounced off towards the changing-room on a complete high. 'We really showed those Tigers today, didn't we?'

'It could have been oh-so-different if Georgie hadn't pulled off that brilliant save in the first half.' Grace swung round to grin at me. 'The girl's a star!'

'I just wish I hadn't let one in right at the very end,' I groaned.

'It wasn't your fault, Georgie,' Katy said earnestly. 'It was a great shot from the Tigers' midfielder.'

'Girls, well done!' Ria called, crossing the field to us. 'That was great teamwork.'

Everyone else stopped and gathered around her, but I turned away and carried on walking off the pitch. I'd ignored Ria at half-time as well. While she'd been giving us a team talk, I'd stared off into the distance and hadn't looked at her once. I was hoping she'd got the message by now.

'Georgie!' I came to a halt at the sound of Dad's voice behind me. Guiltily I turned back. Dad, Adey, Jack and Luke were coming towards me. Dad was looking a little stern, and I knew it was because he'd seen me walk away from Ria.

'Great game, Fishface,' Jack said, giving me a punch on the shoulder.

'You were cool, sister,' Adey told me.

Luke didn't say anything. I didn't really know why he'd bothered to come again today – probably because he just wanted to wind me up about any mistakes, later. Like the goal I'd let in, for instance.

'You played really well, Georgie,' said Dad.

'I thought we could all go out to lunch to celebrate.' He paused, then, looking a bit awkward, he slid his arm around my shoulders. 'And I've invited Ria to come, too.'

Saturday 19th – 4.15pm

WHAT A DISASTER!!! That must have been just about the worst meal ever, for lots of reasons...

Dad took us all to this really posh country pub, and I knew he was doing it just to impress Ria. I had scampi and chips (well, it was called something different on the glossy menu, but that's basically what it was). I couldn't swallow much, though. I was too choked up to eat.

At first, everyone was really quiet. I wasn't speaking to Ria anyway, Dad looked totally awkward, and Luke and Jack were silent and sulky. I was secretly glad though – I knew they didn't really want dad to go out with Ria!

Then Ria and Adey started chatting (I think Adey felt a bit sorry for her – he's just as soft-hearted as Dad). Ria was completely different from how she is with the Stars. I couldn't believe it! She was chatty and smiley and friendly. She and Adey started discussing Melfield United and their promotion hopes for this season, and Ria mentioned that she was hoping to invite several international footballers she knew to come to the Open Day in a week's time. What a name-dropper.

I could see that Luke and Jack were dead impressed, even though they were trying not to show it. By the time Dad ordered dessert, they were occasionally joining in the conversation between Adey, Ria and Dad. They even looked respectful when Ria showed off how much she knew about footie tactics and strategies. I know loads about football, too, so why can't Luke and Jack be nicer to me?

I'd thought it might be difficult for me to keep on ignoring Ria during lunch, but it wasn't. That was because by the end of it, everyone else was talking so much, they were ignoring me. I couldn't *believe* that Luke and Jack had been taken in by Ria pretending to be all friendly...

So I sat there silent and resentful and seething with rage, so upset I couldn't even finish my strawberry cheesecake and ice-cream.

Then, when the others said goodbye to Ria (I didn't, obviously), Dad told her he'd see her tomorrow.

SO HE AND RIA HAVE ANOTHER DATE! This is *bad*.

They *have* to split up. They just have to. And you know what, I'll do whatever it takes...

CHAPTER
EIGHT

'So what happened at lunch yesterday, Georgie?' Jasmin asked, her big brown eyes wide with curiosity. 'I think you've avoided our questions for long enough!'

'All right, all right,' I groaned, holding up my hands. 'I give in. I'll tell you.'

It was Sunday afternoon. Wearing our swimsuits, we were sitting in the bubbling hot tub on the patio of Lauren's frankly gigantic garden. It wasn't a particularly warm day, but once you were in the water, it felt deliciously hot and cosy.

'So are your dad and Ria an item?' Hannah wanted to know.

'Oh, don't start without me!' Lauren wailed, appearing at the French windows with a tray of fizzing drinks, complete with curly straws and little paper parasols. 'Look, Dad's mixed up these cocktails for us.'

'What's in them?' Katy said, taking one of the glasses.

'No idea,' Lauren confessed with a grin. 'But definitely no alcohol!'

She handed the glasses round and then clambered into the hot tub with the rest of us.

'Ooh, this is so *lush*!' Grace sighed, leaning back into the warm bubbles. 'I wish we had one of these at home.'

'It was Mum's idea to buy it,' Lauren told us. 'Dad was a bit annoyed at first – he said it'd be too expensive to run. But now he loves it.'

'Why is *your* dad worrying about it being expensive?' Hannah asked in amazement. 'He's loaded!'

Lauren shrugged. 'Dad loves spending money, but he tries to be all sensible and stern every so often. It doesn't last, though!'

I kept quiet in my corner of the tub, sipping my

fruity, fizzy drink, hoping that they'd forget all about my dad and Ria. No chance!

'Come on, then, Georgie.' Grace turned to look enquiringly at me. 'What's going on?'

'Yes, tell us all,' Lauren chimed in.

I sighed. 'OK. Lunch yesterday was a disaster, and Dad and Ria are going out again tonight. Happy now?'

The others stared solemnly at me.

'Well, you're obviously not,' Hannah remarked. 'Happy, I mean.'

'Would *you* be?' I burst out. 'I admit I don't like Ria—'

'We *had* noticed.' Lauren raised her eyebrows.

'Well, then,' I muttered sulkily. 'So the only question now is, how do I get them to split up?'

When we'd arrived home yesterday after lunch, I'd tried to get Jack and Luke on-side, hoping they'd back me up in my campaign.

'Look, Georgie, Dad's going to go on dates, whether we like it or not,' Jack had retorted with a shrug. 'So it might as well be with someone who's OK, like Ria.'

'Anyway, Dad's girlfriends never last that long,' Luke had pointed out irritably. 'It'll probably be over and finished in five minutes.' He scowled. 'Like me and Chloe.'

So it looked like this was down to me, and me alone.

'Split them up?' Jasmin repeated, her eyes two round Os. 'You're not *serious*, Georgie?'

'Sure I'm serious.' I glanced round at them all. 'Any ideas?'

'We could kidnap Wayne Rooney just before an England game, and demand that Freya return from Dubai and be our coach again,' Jasmin said. 'Otherwise we won't let Wayne play in the match.'

'Nice one, Jasmin.' I aimed a kick at her under the water. 'Sensible suggestions only, please.'

'Maybe Ria isn't really the problem,' Hannah suggested a little nervously. 'Maybe you wouldn't like *anyone* your dad dated, Georgie.'

'That's not true!' I retorted, although secretly I knew that I hadn't reacted very well in the past when Dad had dated other women. 'Anyway, how would *you* like it if it was *your* dad?'

'I wouldn't,' Hannah admitted, patting my shoulder sympathetically.

'You shouldn't get involved, Georgie,' Grace said seriously. 'Things between your dad and Ria will probably just fizzle out anyway.'

I shrugged. 'I'm not going to stand around and take that chance,' I retorted. *Goodie-goodie Grace strikes again!* little devil Georgie whispered in my ear.

'Grace is right, Georgie.' Lauren just *had* to go and stick her nose in too. 'Look, we're only saying this stuff because we care about you.'

'I thought *you* didn't like Ria much either,' I snapped.

'She's OK,' Lauren replied. 'I *still* don't like her as much as Freya. But she knows what she's talking about on the pitch, and now she's starting to relax and get to know us, I think she'll be a good coach.'

'Me too,' Hannah chimed in. 'She's got a great sense of humour, I think, but we're only just starting to see it.'

I shook my head in disgust. Ria had got them all fooled, hadn't she?

'Why don't *you* like Ria, Georgie?'

This unexpected question from Katy threw me off balance.

'What do you mean?' I asked warily.

'What I said.' Katy smiled at me. 'Why don't you like her?'

'It's obvious, isn't it?' I snapped.

'Is it?'

'Ooh, I think I know the answer to this!' Jasmin bounced up and down, splashing us all in the process. 'Georgie doesn't like Ria because *she's* not Freya.'

'That's stupid,' I said, trying to sound all calm and dignified, which was difficult sitting in a bubbly hot tub wearing a tatty old black swimming cossie. 'I don't like Ria because I don't think she's a good coach. And she's too strict. I couldn't imagine going to see her if I'd got a problem.'

'Did you like Freya the first few times you met her?' asked Katy.

'Well, of *course* I did—' I began, but then I stopped abruptly as memories popped into my head. I hadn't liked Freya much when I first joined the Stars years ago because she wanted me to try out in goal. Suddenly I could clearly remember telling my mum how much I hated her!

'Anyway, that's not the point,' I said quickly. 'The point is, I *don't* want Ria going out with my dad. And I'm going to let her know it, too.'

The others gazed at me in silence.

'Is that a good idea, Georgie?' Grace said at last.

'We're only saying all these things because we're your mates, and we don't want you to get into trouble,' Jasmin lectured.

'Trouble?' I scoffed. 'What trouble? Ria can't do anything to me.'

'She could suspend you from the team,' Hannah suggested.

I laughed. 'I'm the only goalie available,' I pointed out. 'Some weeks we don't even have a sub if someone's ill, and then we have to play with ten people, or try to borrow a spare player from the Under-Twelves! Ria won't drop me.'

'Maybe you need to think about this a bit more, Georgie,' Grace said gently. But I just shrugged. The war between me and Ria was on, and I *definitely* intended to win…

Sunday 20th – 5pm

I did something pretty bad.

When I got home from Lauren's, no one else was in, although I knew Dad and Adey would be back soon. I didn't know where the two idiots were!

Anyway, as I took my coat off in the hall, I noticed the answerphone light winking at me. There was a message for Dad from Ria.

Hi, Daniel, can't make our date tonight, I'm afraid. Really sorry! I hope you get this message, I've lost your mobile number – typical me! Give me a call. Ria.

So what did I do? I deleted the message immediately, almost without thinking. The answerphone was just resetting itself when the front door opened. I jumped so high in the air, I almost hit my head on the ceiling.

It was Luke coming home. He stared at me a bit strangely as he took his jacket off, probably because I was bright red and looked really guilty, although he didn't say anything.

I know I shouldn't have done it, and I *did* feel guilty, honest. I felt worse when I watched Dad come home, get ready to meet Ria and go out again. But I'm secretly hoping that Dad'll get annoyed with Ria for standing him up. He's been gone for a couple of hours though, so maybe he met some of his mates and went for a drink. He wouldn't have waited all this time for Ria. Maybe Grace is right and things will just

'Georgie?'

That was Dad calling me from downstairs. I hadn't heard him come in. Quickly I shoved my diary into the washing-basket and ran downstairs. I hoped I didn't look *too* guilty.

Dad was in the hall. To my amazement, so was *Ria*. My stomach lurched. Ria was wearing a floaty, floral dress, heels and a denim jacket, as well as make-up, and she looked much prettier than she did in her tracksuit and trainers, I acknowledged grudgingly.

'Georgia,' Dad began (*full name – you know what THAT means!*). 'Do you know anything about a message Ria left for me earlier this afternoon?'

I was caught. I don't mind telling little white lies occasionally, but I didn't like lying to Dad.

'Georgie deleted it, I think,' Luke called from the living room. 'She was acting really guilty around the answerphone when I got home.'

Dad eyed me sternly. '*Did* you delete it, Georgie?'

Every bit of me was now burning red with embarrassment. 'So?' I mumbled, staring down at my feet. 'It's no big deal, is it?'

'It would have been if Ria hadn't found my mobile number in her sports bag and called me,' Dad said quietly. 'What have you got to say for yourself, Georgia?'

'Sorry,' I replied automatically. But I didn't mean it.

'All right. We'll talk about this again later,' Dad

replied, leaving me in no doubt that he wasn't pleased with me.

I turned without looking at Ria and ran upstairs. I threw myself on my bed, hating my life and everybody in it, but mostly Ria and Luke. Why did Luke have to open his oversized mouth and dump me right in it? And then there was Ria. It was all her fault that I was in trouble with Dad.

No, this is partly your *fault*, little angel Georgie said in one ear. *You shouldn't have deleted that message.*

Don't let them treat you this way, little devil Georgie ordered. *Stand up for yourself!*

And I knew which one I was going to listen to...

'Georgie, what are you *doing*?' Jasmin chased after me, looking so petrified I thought she was going to wet herself. It was Tuesday evening and we were at the first training session of the week. It was also the first time I'd seen Ria since Sunday evening. 'Didn't you hear what Ria *said*?'

'Of course I heard,' I replied with a shrug. 'I'm just not taking any notice of her, that's all.'

I'd started the training session as I meant to go on. When Ria had said *hi* to me, I'd ignored her. I'd hummed away to myself when she was giving us our instructions – quietly, but just loud enough to annoy Ria. I'd only jogged around the pitch while the others were running fast, and I hadn't put any effort into anything. I think I *was* getting on Ria's nerves because she'd already told Jasmin, Jo-Jo and Lauren off for chatting too much, and she was looking edgy and irritated.

We'd spent some time talking about what we were going to do at the Melfield United Open Day this Sunday, and that was really the only time I'd behaved myself so far today. But a few minutes ago Ria had told us to get into pairs to practise controlled heading, and not to waste any more time. I'd hooked up with Jasmin, but after a few headers I'd decided I wanted my chewing gum from the changing-room. So I was strolling off to get it without asking for permission.

Don't get me wrong, I wasn't enjoying doing all this. Yes, I'm stubborn and a loudmouth, but I'm not really *mean*. So why was I doing it? I hardly knew, really. I just couldn't think of another way to let Ria know how much she was upsetting and frustrating me. The other girls seemed to find it much easier to talk about this kind of stuff, but

I didn't. I wouldn't have been able to find the words to explain how I was feeling even if Ria had asked me straight out—

'Georgie!' Ria yelled. But I didn't turn round.

'She's just going to get her chewing gum, Ria,' Jasmin called nervously.

'We've wasted enough time tonight already,' Ria snapped. 'Georgie, come back here.'

I turned round and stared Ria straight in the eye. 'I won't be a minute,' I said.

'Please come back and carry on right away,' Ria replied quietly.

'In a minute,' I repeated.

I was about to turn away again when Ria's next words stopped me in my tracks.

'As things aren't going very well at the moment, Georgie, I think it's better for the team if you don't play this Saturday against the Burnlee Bees. You can sit the next game out.'

CHAPTER NINE

For a moment I thought I was dreaming. There was a stunned silence, and everyone stared at me and at Ria.

'Wh-*what* did you say?' I stammered.

Ria wasn't looking triumphant or pleased that she'd got the better of me. Her face was red and stern and unsmiling, in fact, she looked almost *embarrassed* – as if she'd instantly regretted the words that came out of her mouth. Oh, how well I knew that feeling myself...

'I think we have some issues that need to be sorted

out, Georgie,' Ria said. She was struggling to remain calm, I could see, but my own temper was quickly soaring to boiling point. 'So I think it's best if you don't play this Saturday.'

'But that means we won't have a goalie!' Lauren said anxiously.

'Yes, who'll play in goal?' Hannah fretted.

'You will, Hannah, if you're up for it,' Ria replied. 'Freya told me you've done it before when Georgie was injured.'

The look on Hannah's face would have made me giggle if I hadn't been so utterly torn apart with misery and rage.

'But – I'm rubbish!' Hannah spluttered.

'I'll give you some basic training now, and again on Thursday,' Ria replied shortly, 'Now, everyone get back to what you were doing—'

'It's not fair!' I burst out. 'This isn't what's best for the team!'

Ria gave me a *look*. 'At the moment, this *is* what's best for the team, Georgie,' she said quietly. 'Now go back to Jasmin and—'

'If I'm not playing on Saturday, then I don't need to train, do I?' I yelled. 'And I won't be coming to the Open Day on Sunday, either!'

I turned and ran. I was in the changing-room in seconds, grabbing my clothes, not even bothering to get changed. Then I dashed out to the car park at the front of the college. Dad was sitting in our car, reading his newspaper.

'You're very early,' he remarked, looking mildly surprised as I wrenched the passenger door open.

'I don't need to train today,' I retorted, chucking my bag onto the back seat. 'I've been dropped from the team!'

'Oh?' Dad glanced sideways at me as he started the engine. 'Why's that, then?'

I hesitated. Should I give the correct answer which was *I was really annoying and wound Ria up*, or should I try to get Dad on my side? Little devil Georgie won.

'Ria doesn't like me,' I snapped, sinking down into my seat.

'That's not true, Georgie.' Dad edged out of the car park into the traffic. 'She wouldn't have dropped you from the team without good reason.'

'Why are you always on *her* side?' I demanded bitterly. Somehow it was easier to have this kind of conversation with Dad in the car. He didn't have to look at me, and I didn't have to look at him. We could both just stare straight ahead, which is exactly what we did.

I even went one step further and said something I'd never have dared say before.

'*Why* are you going out with her, Dad? I'd never have believed that you'd date someone I didn't like...'

There was a tense silence, and I wondered if I'd gone too far. But when Dad spoke, his voice was gentle.

'Georgie, if I really and truly believed that you didn't like Ria for very good reasons, of course I'd think extremely seriously about getting to know her better. But I'm convinced there's more to this than meets the eye. This is about Freya leaving, as much as it's about Ria.'

'No, it isn't,' I mumbled.

'I think it is,' Dad went on. 'You need to let Freya go, sweetheart, and give Ria a chance to prove herself to you, and to the team.' He sighed. 'I know it's difficult when people we love go out of our lives, for whatever reason. Dealing with changes we don't like is never easy...'

I stared out of the window, struggling to control my feelings.

Your dad's talking sense, little angel Georgie told me. *Listen to him.*

Look what Ria's done now! little devil Georgie ranted. *Your dad's on her side, against you, so what are you going to do about it?*

Wednesday 23rd – 4.40pm

God, what a day! I couldn't stop thinking about what happened last night. I'm not that great a student anyway, but I hit an all-time low today in most of my classes.

Maths was *really* bad because that's my worst subject. I *totally* got all my sums wrong, even though Katy, who's in my group, was trying to help me. Miss Burton rolled her eyes and told me in this really snotty voice that I was NEVER going to understand numbers. So I just said in that case, I'd use a calculator, and Miss Burton totally went off on one! She hates it when anyone says stuff like that – I think she'd like calculators to be banned!

After the last few weeks, I think Miss Burton now officially hates me!

Anyway, the girls are all on my side. Sort of. I got loads of texts and calls after the training session last night, and I talked about it today at school with

Grace, Hannah and Katy. It was a six-way conversation, really, because Lauren and Jasmin were joining in by text! They really want me to play on Saturday. So do I, and I don't want to miss the Open Day on Sunday. The only problem is, the girls think I should apologise to Ria...

Like I'm going to do that.

But no worries, because I've come up with what I think is a brilliant and foolproof idea! I've asked all the girls to meet me in our usual place at the park tonight. I need their help, and I'm sure they'll say YES...

'So what's going on, Georgie?' Katy called, hurrying towards us as we sat perched on our favourite bench. She was last to arrive, ten minutes later than everyone else. 'I can't stay long. I have to be home in half an hour.'

'Me, too.' Jasmin glanced nervously at her watch. 'The oldies don't like me coming out on a school night.'

'And I've still got a load of homework to do,' Lauren groaned.

'Well, if you lot stop talking, I'll tell you my brilliant idea right away.' I jumped to my feet. 'Come on, let's walk.'

'What brilliant idea is this, then?' Grace wanted to know.

'Just think about it,' I began as we wandered along the path towards the football pitches. 'How many of us are there?'

'Is this a trick question?' Jasmin asked suspiciously. 'There's six of us, or there was last time I looked!'

'And how many people in a football team?' I went on.

'This is freaking me out,' Lauren remarked. 'What *are* you getting at, Georgie?'

'How many in a football team?' I insisted.

'Eleven,' the others chorused.

'Exactly!' I beamed at them. 'Six is more than half of eleven, isn't it?'

'Yes,' Katy agreed. 'Your maths isn't *that* bad.'

'So without us six, there *is* no Stars Under-Thirteens team,' I pointed out. 'JoJo, Debs and the others couldn't play without us.'

The girls looked puzzled.

'But *we* haven't been dropped,' Grace said.

'I know,' I replied impatiently. 'But if you five go on strike—'

'STRIKE?' they all repeated, looking shocked.

'Then there *is* no team,' I finished triumphantly. 'You go to Ria and tell her you won't play either unless I'm back in the team. What do you reckon?' Silence.

'God, this is a tough one,' Lauren said at last. 'We all want it sorted, but is *this* the best way, Georgie?'

'Why not?' I demanded. 'No us, no team.'

It was the perfect solution, as far as I could see. Although the Stars did have some girls who played occasionally when we couldn't, there were only two or three of them. Sometimes we borrowed players from the Under-Twelves team, but they didn't have that many spare either. In the past we'd even played the odd match with fewer then eleven players, but then you had to hope the other team would agree to do the same – and they didn't *have* to! Anyway, even when that'd happened, we'd *still* had nine or ten players – but this Saturday Ria would only have five, if everything went to plan. That just wasn't enough. Also, the club got fined sometimes if they couldn't put out a full team for a fixture, and I was sure Ria wouldn't want that. She'd *have* to reinstate me.

'You could just apologise to Ria, Georgie—' Katy began.

'No,' I said. 'She shouldn't have dropped me. Freya wouldn't have.'

'You *were* being annoying, Georgie,' Grace said quietly. 'Freya wouldn't have let you get away with doing that, either.'

'Ria's going out with my dad!' I snapped. 'How would you like *that* if you were me?'

Grace sighed. 'I wouldn't like it one bit,' she admitted.

'So will you guys do it?' I asked as we neared the football pitches.

The girls looked at each other.

'Just charging up to Ria and saying we're going on strike seems a bit over the top,' Hannah said cautiously. She glanced enquiringly at Grace, Katy, Lauren and Jasmin. 'How about if the five of us go and *ask* her to put Georgie back in the team first?'

'That's a good idea,' Grace agreed. 'Going on strike would be an absolute last resort.' And the others nodded.

'Thanks, you lot,' I said gratefully.

'But you're going to have to sort things out with Ria sometime, Georgie,' Lauren said severely. 'You can't carry on like *this* for the rest of the season—'

'Hey, it's the Purple Petunias!'

We all glanced round. Luke and Jack were on one of the football pitches, booting a ball to each other. They stopped and grinned at us.

'Oh, I'm not in the mood for those two braindead boneheads today,' I muttered. 'Ignore them.'

We walked on, but Luke and Jack came after us.

'So which one's Grace?' Jack yelled. Grace paused, looking surprised, and glanced round at them.

'Oh, yeah, that's her!' Luke said triumphantly. 'She's the goodie-goodie who's so sweet and nice, it's *sickening*. And she sticks her nose into everyone else's business too!'

'Katy does that as well, doesn't she?' Jack remarked. 'The quiet, mysterious and moody one who *thinks* she's so mature and drives everyone nuts?'

Grace and Katy had both turned pink and were looking angry.

'What *are* they talking about?' asked Katy, frowning.

'Run along and play, boys,' Lauren called.

Luke turned to Jack. 'Which one is *she*?'

'I've got it!' Jack was grinning from ear to ear. 'She's the rich one who spends a fortune on a load

170

of rubbish – the one whose parents have got more money than sense!'

Lauren gasped. 'What the hell's going on?' she spluttered, outraged.

I didn't answer her. I *couldn't*. I'd just realised that these rude comments Jack and Luke were making sounded all too horribly familiar…

'So who's left?' Luke wondered aloud. 'Oh, yes, I can't remember her name – but there's one who's so daft, she always falls over her feet and gives away goals, isn't there?'

'Ooh, that's me!' Jasmin squealed indignantly.

'And then there's Hannah – the milkshake traitor with the big mouth!' Jack added. He and Luke were almost helpless with laughter by this stage and could hardly stand up.

'You nasty little creeps!' I yelled. 'That was all private – you had no right to read it!'

'Read what?' Hannah demanded, her face flushed and furious.

'My diary!' The words were out of my mouth before I could stop myself. There was a moment of tense silence as we stared at each other.

'*You* wrote all that stuff about us?' Lauren said coldly.

'That's so mean, Georgie!' Jasmin was nearly in tears.

'Oh, come on, Jasmin,' I began nervously. 'We've laughed over you being clumsy *loads* of times.'

'Yes, but it's different with *mates*,' Jasmin retorted. 'It was spiteful to write it in your diary and let your horrible brothers read it!' And she stormed off. Throwing me a *look*, Grace went after her.

'I didn't *let* them read it!' I protested, feeling sick to my stomach. Luke and Jack had picked up their football and strolled off, still smirking. I was going to kill the pair of them when I got home, I swear.

I turned to Hannah, Lauren and Katy. 'I wrote lots of nice stuff, too, you know—'

'Forget it,' Lauren snapped, turning on her heel, 'And stuff the strike, too! You're on your own, Georgie.'

'Yes, I'll be playing in goal on Saturday, and I don't care if I *am* rubbish!' Hannah added.

Then she, Katy and Lauren walked off too, leaving me all alone.

CHAPTER TEN

'WHERE ARE YOU, YOU SLIMY, SPYING LITTLE TOADS?' I yelled. I slammed the front door behind me and charged into the living room. Dad and Adey were sprawled on the sofas watching the news, and they both looked at me, eyebrows raised.

'Luke and Jack went into my room and read my private diary!' I gabbled, so furious and upset I could hardly get the words out. 'They told all my friends what I'd written, and it was *really* embarrassing!'

Dad frowned. He grabbed the remote and pressed *mute*. 'Jack! Luke! Get down here RIGHT NOW!' he shouted.

We heard footsteps clattering down the stairs and then the boys appeared in the doorway. They were still smiling just a bit, and I wanted to *slap* them.

'Take those smirks off your faces when I'm talking to you,' Dad said sternly. 'Did one or both of you go into Georgie's room and read her diary?'

Both of them shook their heads.

'I found it on the kitchen floor under the table,' Luke protested.

'That's a lie!' I burst out.

'Let me handle this, Georgie,' Dad said. 'Is that the truth?'

Luke and Jack nodded.

'You couldn't have done!' I snapped. 'It was hidden in my washing basket!'

'Ah...' Dad suddenly looked very embarrassed. 'Now I see what *might* have happened. I know we usually do our own washing, but I noticed your basket was very full this morning, Georgie, so I took a load of stuff out to put in the machine with some of mine.'

'There you go, then,' Luke said with a grin. 'Dad must have pulled the diary out with the clothes and it fell onto the kitchen floor while he was loading the washing-machine. Simple!'

'So?' I yelled, boiling with rage. 'You still shouldn't have *read* it!'

'Georgie's right,' Dad agreed. 'So let's discuss how you two can make it up to her. Firstly, you can apologise for embarrassing her in front of her friends. Secondly, you can spend some of your savings to buy her a new diary – with a *padlock* – and thirdly, you can take over *all* her chores in the house for the next two weeks...'

But I was still boiling with rage even after Luke and Jack had muttered an apology. It served those two clowns right, but they weren't my biggest problem right now. At the moment I *wasn't* playing for the Stars on Saturday, I *wasn't* going to the Open Day on Sunday and I *didn't* have any footie mates any more. The worst thing of all was that I had seen how hurt and upset the other girls were by the thoughtless things I'd written about them. It was all stuff we'd said to each other before, either teasingly or in the heat of furious arguments, but somehow it had sounded so much worse when Luke and Jack said it all out loud...

Now I was alone and my life had gone way off track. Somehow I had to sort things out.

Thursday 24th – 4.30pm

I'm not really sure I want to write in this diary any more. Now that I know Luke and Jack have been reading it, it feels kind of – weird. Maybe I'll feel differently when I get my new padlocked diary. But anyway, at the moment, my diary's really the only friend I've got...

How sad am I?

Just got back from school, which was HORRIBLE. Grace, Hannah and Katy avoided me all day. It wasn't difficult for them to do because we don't have many lessons together on Thursdays. But they didn't wait for me at lunchtime like they usually did, and they didn't speak to me at break time, either. I just wanted to explain everything, but they didn't give me a chance. I did text SORRY to all of them, but I got no replies.

So I guess there's only one thing for it. I'm going to have to apologise and apologise BIG, to get things sorted. That means face to face, so I'll have to go to the training session tonight. Maybe Ria will chuck me out, though. God, what a mess...

'This looks serious,' Adey said lightly as he drove into the car park. Grace, Hannah, Katy, Lauren and Jasmin were standing on the steps of the college building, staring at us. 'Do you want me to hang around for a bit?'

'No, I'll be fine,' I muttered. 'You go, or you'll be late meeting your girlfriend.'

As Adey drove off, I headed straight towards the others. I knew *exactly* what I had to do.

'Look, guys, I'm really, *really* sorry,' I said as I reached the steps. 'I know some of those things Luke and Jack said were a bit harsh, but it was only really stuff we've said to each other before. And,' I swallowed nervously, 'they didn't tell you any of the *fab* things I wrote about you all, and how much I love being part of the gang. I'd hate for those two idiots to spoil everything.' *God, I wasn't going to cry, was I? That would be sooo embarrassing!*

'It's OK, Georgie,' Jasmin said quickly. 'We've all calmed down a bit now.'

'We *were* pretty annoyed, though,' Grace admitted. 'I'm glad you've said sorry.'

'And, Georgie, if you're going to keep a secret diary in future, make sure it *is* a secret,' Hannah added with a faint grin.

'So we're cool?' I asked, relief flooding through me.

'The coolest!' Lauren slapped me on the back, and Katy nodded.

'And the strike's still on, then?' I said eagerly.

The girls glanced at each other.

'Actually, Georgie, we talked about the strike and we really don't think it's such a great idea,' Lauren said in a very serious tone.

'What!' I exclaimed.

'We don't think it's good for the team for *all* of us to be fighting with Ria,' Grace explained.

'But we'll go and see her and ask if you can play on Saturday,' Katy assured me.

'You might have to apologise though, and promise to try and get along with her a bit better,' Jasmin said earnestly.

But little devil Georgie was whispering in my ear again. 'No chance!' I snapped. Then, to make my point, I turned and walked swiftly out of the car park. I regretted it bitterly before I'd even reached the gates, but I wouldn't give in, even when I heard the girls calling me. I'm stubborn, as you may have realised by now...

Why did I do this stuff? I asked myself miserably as I caught the bus home. I was my own worst enemy in some ways. *Would* it be so difficult for me to try and get along with Ria? So what if she and Dad went out occasionally? Why did it matter so much?

Everything seemed one huge, tangled mess. Ria, Dad, Luke, Jack, Mum, Rainbow, the girls... I thought my head was going to explode as I let myself into the house.

'Anyone home?' I called shakily. Silence. I knew that Dad was working late, Adey had gone to meet his girlfriend and Jack was in town with his mates. Luke must be out, too. I was all alone.

I shut the front door and suddenly, just like that, I began to cry. Tears rolled down my cheeks, one after the other. They were unstoppable. I just stood there and sobbed. I hadn't cried like this since Mum died...

I went into the living room, flung myself onto the sofa, buried my head in a cushion and howled. Suddenly I heard footsteps coming downstairs. A few seconds later, Luke appeared in the doorway. He stopped and stared at me. I'd never felt so embarrassed in my *life*, but still the tears kept coming.

'I-I didn't think there was anyone h-home,' I gulped.

'I was in my bedroom with my headphones on.' Luke came a little way into the room, looking wary. 'What's up?'

'N-n-nothing!' I wailed. Probably the most stupid

answer to a question, ever.

Luke didn't say anything. He turned, and I heard him go down the hall to the kitchen. *Typical*, I thought bitterly, still gulping and wiping my face. *He doesn't even care.* But I felt ashamed of myself when Luke came back with a glass of water and a box of tissues.

'Here,' he said, thrusting the tissues at me, still looking completely embarrassed.

Silently I wiped my face. I was glad of the water too, because I'd been crying so hard I'd got hiccups.

'Thanks,' I muttered when I'd got myself cleaned up and under control again.

Luke cleared his throat and sat down next to me. 'So what's up? I've never seen you like this before. Except—' He stopped.

'When Mum died?' I filled in the gap for him.

'Yes.' We were silent for a minute. 'You're so tough, usually, Georgie.'

'Is that what you think?' I said, almost managing a cynical smile. I'd obviously done a good job at hiding my real feelings.

'Well, aren't you?' Luke looked surprised. 'You never let me and Jack get away with *anything*.'

'I can't,' I retorted quite sharply. 'My life would be hell if I did!'

Luke looked completely taken aback. 'What do you mean?'

'You *know* what I mean,' I said. 'You and Jack are always ganging up on me and teasing me and saying nasty things—'

Luke looked so shocked, I almost felt sorry for him. 'But it's just us messing around!' he exclaimed. 'OK, the diary thing was a bit mean...' He looked a little ashamed of himself. 'I was still so mad about what happened with Chloe.'

'But I didn't do that on purpose!' I broke in. 'I honestly *didn't* know you'd split up with Lucy. And I never met her, so I just assumed Chloe was her.' My voice wobbled a little as I went on 'You don't really think I could be *that* spiteful do you?'

Luke hesitated.

'You do!' I accused him. 'You don't really know me at all, do you?'

'Well, I could say the same thing about you!' Luke retorted, his face turning red. 'Jack and I are only mucking about and teasing you most of the time—'

'Oh, so you *didn't* start coming to my matches just to give me a hard time, then?' I said sarcastically. 'That's more than a bit of light-hearted teasing, isn't it?'

Luke stared at me in surprise. '*Dad* asked me and Jack to come.'

'What!' This was news to me.

'He said it'd be good to do more as a family,' Luke explained. 'I think he was hoping it might help us get along better. You know how sick he is of us arguing all the time. Anyway, it wasn't mine or Jack's idea.'

I stared suspiciously at him. 'And you and Jack just gave in and did what Dad said, like good little boys? Come off it, Luke, I'm not daft!'

Luke looked extremely sheepish. 'Well, he *did* promise us a new Xbox...'

I burst out laughing, I couldn't help it. But it was good to know that my brothers *hadn't* come along to the games to try and annoy me. I'd just jumped to conclusions.

'Look, Georgie, Jack and me don't *mean* anything horrible with all this teasing. And, anyway, you give as good as you get...' Luke's voice trailed away as I stopped laughing and my face fell.

'Because I feel like if I don't, I'll go under!' I sighed. 'Sometimes it seems you two don't even *like* me.'

Luke jumped up and began to pace around the

room. 'But we're just treating you like a brother!' he said, looking puzzled. 'Jack and me wind each other up all the time, and we take the mick out of Adey, too. It's no different.'

'But *I'm* different,' I said. 'I'm NOT your brother. I'm your sister!'

'You don't act like it,' Luke pointed out.

'OK, so it's partly my fault, too,' I admitted reluctantly. 'I thought the only way I could get along in this family was by being louder and more stubborn than everyone else.'

'Yeah, I know what you mean,' Luke agreed. 'It can be a bit of a madhouse sometimes, can't it? I think that's what Mum meant when she said—'

'What?' I asked curiously. 'What did Mum say?'

Luke gazed down at his feet. 'Oh, just before she died, she asked me, Jack and Adey to look after you,' he said quietly.

'She did?' I felt tears begin to slide slowly down my face again.

Luke nodded. 'She said it'd be hard for you, being the only girl. It was easier for Adey to do it because he's older, I guess, but whenever Jack and I tried, you were like *Get off! Leave me alone! I can do it myself!*'

I knew that what Luke was saying was true. All of a sudden I could see very clearly that after Mum died I'd become louder and more stubborn and more rebellious to hide my feelings of grief and hurt. I'd pushed my brothers away, and only Adey had been grown-up and mature enough to cope with me. Luke and Jack had had no chance. All they'd done was treat me the way they thought I *wanted* to be treated.

'I'm sorry,' I said. I hated saying those words to *anyone* because it meant I was in the wrong! But now they came more easily to me than they ever had before.

'Me, too.' Luke grinned at me, and this time I could really *see* the affection in his face. Maybe it had always been there, and I'd just never noticed it until now. 'Is this the bit where we have a big hug and live happily ever after?'

'Are you mad?' I grabbed another tissue and mopped my face. 'This isn't a fairy-tale! You and Jack are still going to annoy me, and we're still going to argue—'

'And you're *definitely* going to annoy us, too!' Luke retorted. We smiled at each other. There was a real sense that we'd cleared the air between us, and it felt *great*. 'You OK now?'

I nodded. Luke bounded out of the room, humming to himself, and looking as if a ton weight had been lifted off his shoulders. I felt *exactly* the same way.

I turned the TV on and lay down on the sofa, feeling exhausted but in a good way. If this was how it felt to get emotional issues sorted out, maybe it *was* time for me to speak to Ria face to face... But was I ready to take that enormous step?

I must have dozed off because the ring of the doorbell jerked me awake. Yawning, I glanced at the clock. I'd been lying there for about an hour!

Guessing that Jack had forgotten his key, as usual, I hauled myself sleepily to my feet. I wondered if Luke would tell Jack what had happened tonight, I mused, as I went to the door. I hoped he did. It would be brilliant to get along better with *all* my brothers, not just Adey. Not that I was expecting a miracle – as I told Luke, we were still going to get on each other's nerves most of the time!

I opened the front door, expecting to see Jack.

There stood Ria.

CHAPTER ELEVEN

Ria looked as embarrassed as I felt. We stared at each other in silence for a moment or two.

'Hello, Georgie,' Ria began. Then she peered more closely at me. 'Are you all right?'

I guessed my face was still tear-stained and my eyes a bit red and puffy.

'I'm fine,' I muttered. 'Dad's not here.'

'It's you I want to see,' Ria replied. 'Can I come in?'

I opened the door wider, she came in and we went into the living room. Neither of us sat down.

'I just wanted to say thanks for the note,' Ria said awkwardly. 'It was good of you to apologise, and

I want you to know that—'

'What note?' I asked, confused.

'The note you sent me tonight—' Ria stopped, her eyebrows shooting up. 'It wasn't from you, was it?' she sighed. 'I had my suspicions right from the start.'

She took a note from her jacket pocket and passed it to me. I suppose I was still feeling a little dazed and sleepy because I hadn't guessed yet what was going on. I took the note and read it:

Dear Ria,

I just wanted to say that I'm sorry for everything I've done over the last few weeks. I'd really like to play on Saturday, if that's OK with you.

Georgie

'That's not my writing,' I said, as realisation began to dawn on me. 'But it *does* look like Grace's!'

'Like I said, I *was* a bit taken aback when Lauren gave it to me,' Ria confessed. 'It just didn't seem very likely—' She stopped.

'That I'd apologise?' I muttered. 'Thanks a lot.'

'But I hoped you *would*,' Ria said firmly. 'You're an excellent goalie, Georgie, and I really want you in the team.'

I was surprised but pleased.

'That's why I came here, even though I had my suspicions about the note not being genuine,' Ria added. 'It gives me a chance to talk to you, and clear the air.'

Clear the air... It had worked with Luke and made me feel better. But could it work with Ria? For the first time since I'd met her, I wasn't feeling so edgy, stressed and wound up. The talk with Luke had left me too emotionally exhausted for all that. I didn't want to keep up the battle any more, I realised. It was doing my head in.

'Your behaviour wasn't acceptable, Georgie, but I don't feel I handled the situation very well, either,' Ria went on. Her frankness made me blink. I hadn't expected *that*. 'I realise now how close you were to Freya. I didn't make allowances for that—'

'I was a brat,' I broke in. If Ria could be honest, then so could I. 'I'm kind of always a *bit* of a brat. But I went over the top.'

Ria nodded. 'Let's face it, Georgie, if we both want what's best for the Stars – and I know we *do* – then we're on the same side, aren't we?'

'Yep,' I said. I took a deep breath. 'I'm sorry.'

There! little angel Georgie said in my ear, *that*

wasn't so bad, was it?

'Me, too. Look, can we forget about it and start all over again?' Ria said. Her direct, open gaze suddenly reminded me of Freya. Maybe I'd never like Ria as much, but did that mean I couldn't like her *at all*? Not even a little bit? For the first time I acknowledged to myself that Freya wasn't coming back. So I had to sink or swim with Ria, or bail out of the team altogether.

'OK,' I agreed, wondering what I was letting myself in for.

Ria held out her hand, and we shook on it. The tension between us had eased slightly, but there was still one thing we hadn't discussed. *Dad.*

As I showed Ria to the door, I silently and painfully came to the realisation that the relationship between Ria and Dad was, like Adey had pointed out, something out of my control. But I'm no angel, as you know! So, even though I'd agreed to try and get along with Ria, I'd still be watching and waiting to see what happened between the two of them. And little devil Georgie *did* point out that it'd be a lot easier to keep an eye on what was going on if I was friendlier with Ria...

But right now I had something else to figure out.

Like how I was going to have a little fun at the other girls' expense, and pay them back (in a nice way!) for interfering!

The first brilliant thing that happened the next morning, before we all went off to school, was that Jack presented me with my new, lockable diary. Luke told me he and Jack went late night shopping yesterday and spent ages looking for a really nice one. Bless!

Of course, Jack started winding me up about what I was going to write in it. Luke tried not to join in, but he only lasted about seven seconds! But somehow I could handle it all *sooo* much better.

'So are you going to write about your totally cool brothers, then?' Jack asked me as he handed the diary over.

'If you mean Adey, then yes,' I replied.

'Ooh, cutting!' Luke said, rolling his eyes. 'I'm so hurt.'

'You two should be nice to me from now on,' I said breezily. 'Because when I'm an England international and I publish my diaries, everyone will know how mean you were to your dear little sister!'

'You reckon you can make it as a professional goalie then, George?' Jack scoffed.

'Course I can,' I replied.

'You ought to be practising all the time, then, not just with the Petunias!' Jack retorted. 'How come you never have a kick-around with me and Luke?'

'You've never asked me,' I replied.

'You've never *asked*,' Jack pointed out.

I've always secretly wished my brothers would let me join in when they're messing around with a football, but I was too proud just to *ask* if I could. I'm beginning to see now that I've been a bit of an idiot in some ways...

At school today, I even got all my fractions right in my maths lesson, and Miss Burton almost fainted on the spot. That'll show *her*!

But the *funniest* thing was when I met up with Grace, Hannah and Katy in the playground this morning. I walked up to them all gloomy and grumpy, and I could see them glancing at each other with concern.

'Sorry I ran off last night, guys.' I heaved a sigh. 'I shouldn't have asked you to go on strike. It wasn't fair.'

'So, has Ria been in touch with you, Georgie?' Hannah asked, a bit too casually.

'Nope.' I shook my head, looking confused. 'Why

would she have contacted me?' *Ha ha ha!*

Oh, the looks on their faces were *priceless*! I knew that once I was out of the way, they'd be frantically texting Lauren and Jasmin to tell them that their little plan hadn't worked.

But I had one more surprise for them up my sleeve!

'Hey, you lot!'

I'd made sure that I was last to arrive at the park that evening for our pre-match get-together. I bounced down the path towards 'our' bench, a big grin splitting my face almost in two. 'Have I got some *brilliant* news for you all!'

'You're back in the team, aren't you?' Jasmin yelled, beaming with relief. 'I *knew* Ria would ask you to play on Saturday after all!'

'That's great, Georgie!' Grace jumped up and gave me a big hug.

'It means I don't have to be goalie – and believe me, I'm not sorry!' Hannah sighed, looking even more relieved than the others.

'So what happened?' Katy asked, a *really* innocent look on her face. 'Did Ria come and see you?'

'Did you apologise to her?' added Lauren.

'What?' I frowned. 'What are you lot twittering

on about? No, Ria *hasn't* been to see me – and of course I haven't apologised!'

As one, the girls' faces all dropped. God, it was *so* funny – I was dying to laugh!

'So why are you bouncing around looking like you've won the lottery?' Lauren demanded.

'Well, when I got home from school this afternoon, I had a call from the coach of the Blackbridge Belles Under-Thirteens,' I explained. 'You'll never guess what – he's offered me a place in their team!'

'WHAT!' the others shouted.

I had to bite the inside of my mouth to stop myself from bursting into giggles. 'Yes, he said he'd always rated me as a goalie, and that it was time I played for a decent team, so—'

'Georgie, I don't *believe* you!' Grace gasped. 'You *can't* be thinking of playing for our biggest rivals?'

I shrugged. 'Well, if Ria doesn't want me—'

'You can't do it, Georgie!' Lauren declared.

I tried to hold myself together, but the looks of outrage on their faces were just too much. I collapsed into hysterics, laughing so hard I had to sit down on the grass.

'Georgie, you lying little scumbag!' Hannah

howled, rushing over to grab me in a headlock.

'Right, you're going to pay for *that*, Georgia Taylor!' Lauren joined Hannah and began to tickle my ribs.

'Stop!' I yelped, crying with laughter.

'Oh!' Jasmin gasped, as Grace and Katy ran over to join the attack. 'It's not true, then?'

'Course it isn't!' I said, managing to pull myself free. 'I wouldn't leave you crazy guys for the Belles, would I? No way! I was just getting my own back for that note you sent Ria!'

'But it worked, didn't it?' Katy asked eagerly. 'You're back in the team?'

I nodded, and there was a round of cheers.

'I *did* say sorry to Ria, and she apologised to me too,' I told them. 'This is the new, improved Georgie Taylor you're looking at, girls!'

'Well, I have to say she looks as much of a mess as the old one did,' Lauren replied, raising her eyebrows at my old trackie bottoms and washed-out T-shirt.

'And that's why I'm going to let you give me that makeover after all!' I shot back with a huge grin.

Well, why not? Everything seemed to be changing around me – for the better – so maybe it was time for me to change, too.

CHAPTER TWELVE

'Not too much stuff on my face,' I said nervously, as Lauren unzipped her make-up bag, looking like she was facing the biggest challenge she'd ever come across in her life so far.

'Don't you trust me?' Lauren said with a grin, waving the mascara tube at me. We were in her funky cream and purple bedroom, me sitting in front of a huge mirror, and the others sprawled on the bed and on beanbags. Chelsea was asleep at my feet, snuffling in her sleep. 'It'll be fine – you'll love it.'

'You look fabulous already, Georgie,' Jasmin

called, handing round the cheese and onion crisps. 'But you're going to look even more stunning with a bit of slap!'

I sneaked yet another glance at myself in the mirror. Dad had given me some money to spend, and we'd gone shopping after the game yesterday. I'd allowed the others to 'persuade' me to buy the turquoise and white striped T-shirt dress we'd seen the day we met Luke and Chloe in the mall. They'd also bullied me into buying some skinny jeans, a wide brown belt, flat white shoes and a white headband. I was wearing the whole outfit now, and even I could see I looked good. Cool, but not too girlie. I'd never spent so much money on clothes all at once in my life (except maybe school uniform!).

We'd won the match yesterday against the Burnlee Bees 1-0 – YAY! Three more points! I'd been a bit nervous about how things would go with Ria, but it was OK, I guess. I tried not to get all edgy when I saw her talking to Dad, and mostly I managed to cope with it. The best thing was, Luke and Jack came to the match because they wanted to, not because Dad told them to, and I could hear them cheering when I pulled off a couple of saves. Grace got the winning goal, but we left it a bit late – she only scored five minutes before the end!

'There.' Lauren slid the top back onto the lip pencil. 'Take a look, Georgie.'

The others whooped with glee and crowded around me as I swung back to the mirror and stared at myself. To my surprise I looked different – much prettier – but I could hardly see any make-up at all.

'Told you, didn't I?' Lauren said with satisfaction. 'You don't need loads of make-up to look good. And I can teach you how to do it yourself, Georgie.'

'Girls?' Mrs Bell was calling from downstairs. 'It's time to leave for the Melfield United Open Day.'

I reached for the packet of face wipes on the dressing table, but Grace grabbed my wrist.

'And what do you think *you're* doing?' she demanded.

'Getting ready for the Open Day,' I retorted. 'I can't go like *this*, can I? I need to change, and—'

Katy took the face wipes from me. 'We can change into our kit at the ground.'

'I didn't mean my kit,' I said defensively, 'I meant put my *own* clothes on.' And I glanced over at my Spurs shirt and black tracksuit hanging on the back of Lauren's door.

'These *are* your own clothes!' Hannah said, pointing at my new outfit.

'You want me to go to the Open Day like this?' I exclaimed, suddenly feeling very nervous. 'Luke and Jack will laugh their heads off.'

'So?' Grace shrugged. 'Sure they'll tease you, but who cares? You look gorgeous.'

'I dare you, Georgie,' Jasmin said, her eyes dancing with mischief.

I hesitated.

'Oh, all right then,' I groaned.

I never could resist a challenge!

The Melfield United Open Day was clearly already a big success by the time we arrived in Mr and Mrs Bell's cars about half an hour after it opened. We were a bit late because the traffic was really bad. The car park in front of the stadium was already full, and we had to park on the road and then queue to get through the gates.

'Relax, Georgie!' Hannah whispered as she caught me tugging nervously at my dress. I just wasn't used to wearing one. Thank goodness I had jeans on too – I wasn't getting my legs out for *anyone!*

There were some stalls selling second-hand junky

type stuff, books and football-related memorabilia around the edges of the car park and at the sides of the stadium, as well as vans selling burgers, chips, baked spuds and drinks. But most of the stalls were on the large field behind the stadium where the club held a car boot sale every Sunday morning. As we made our way over to the field with Lauren's parents, I noticed quite a few of the Melfield United first-team players wandering around having their photos taken with fans. I knew that some of the apprentices, including Adey, were giving guided tours inside the stadium.

'That must be where we're playing our exhibition match,' Lauren said, pointing to an area of the field that had been roped off.

'Maybe we'd better go and get changed,' I suggested, glancing at my watch. We had plenty of time, really, and I did want to look at some of the stalls, especially the ones selling football stuff, but I was desperate to get out of my fancy new clothes before Luke and Jack spotted me.

'Girls! Over here!'

We all turned to see Ria striding towards us. With her were my Dad, Luke and Jack. Turning bright red (not a good look with turquoise!) I slipped behind

Grace and ducked my head, trying to hide.

'Good to see you all here,' Ria said approvingly, after she'd said hello to Mr and Mrs Bell. 'Alicia and the others have arrived, too, so we'll be able put out a full team against Melfield Girls.'

'I thought my daughter would be here with you,' Dad said to Lauren's parents, 'But it looks like Georgie's not coming, and a rather gorgeous young lady's taken her place instead.'

'*Dad!*' I wailed, almost dying with embarrassment.

'Yeah, she's a lot better-looking than Georgie,' Luke said, nudging Jack, and they both sniggered.

'You two are so dead,' I retorted, but I did manage a smile. I think I got off pretty lightly, to be honest!

'Shame you missed the opening, Georgie,' Ria said, smiling at me – a bit warily, but hey, I couldn't really blame her. 'Ray Hilton agreed to come at the last minute and give a speech – you know Ray, the former England goalie? He played in the Melfield youth teams as a schoolboy. He's still around somewhere. I can introduce you if you like?'

'Thanks,' I said, straining to sound suitably grateful. I'd love to meet Ray Hilton, but I still couldn't pretend that *everything* was perfect between me and Ria.

The exhibition match was huge fun. We'd already agreed with Melfield Girls that we'd use the opportunity to show off some of our special skills, and that day at the Brazilian soccer school came in very handy. Jasmin even got cheered for her fabulous heel flicks! The audience were really enthusiastic and I got lots of applause for some really not very special saves. I think some people were just amazed to see girls playing football at all. I noticed Ria and the other coaches giving out leaflets about both clubs – maybe we *would* get a few more players out of it.

After the match, it was time for me to get shot at by members of the public! The coaches were running the stall and taking the money, and the Stars and Melfield goalies took turns between the posts. I was about halfway down the list, so I got to have a wander around the stalls with the girls first before it was my slot.

'Come and score against Georgie, the Stars' goalie!' called Ria to the families walking past as I waited in the goal. The girls were hanging around too, keen to cheer me on. 'Best of three! Under-tens only though, please.'

'Shame,' called Luke. He and Jack had magically

appeared from nowhere now it was my turn between the sticks. Typical! 'I fancied a go myself.'

'Well, you *do* act like a five-year-old, so maybe Ria will let you have a go?' I said sweetly. Jack burst out laughing, so did the girls, and even Luke grinned.

There was a steady stream of kids wanting to take penalties against me. Quite a few of them skied the ball way over the goal, leaving me nothing to do, but I did make a few good saves, the best strikers being girls from the Stars' Under-Eights and Under-Nines teams! I got a few laughs too when some toddlers had a go by pretending to trip over my feet so that they could score.

The last one before my turn was over was a fragile-looking little girl with long dark hair. Surprisingly, she blasted one past me into the corner of my net, and I only just managed to tip her second shot around the post.

'You're really good,' I told her when I'd scooped up her weaker third shot. 'Why don't you try out for the Stars?'

The girl nodded eagerly so I ran over to Ria to get her a leaflet. Ria was talking to a man with cropped dark hair and cool designer specs who looked vaguely familiar. I suddenly realised who it was. Ray

Hilton, the England international goalie!'

'Georgie, I'm sure you know who this is?' Ria said, raising her eyebrows as I skidded to a halt in front of them.

I nodded. I was speechless, just for once!

'I was about to bring Ray over to you,' Ria went on, as Grace, Jasmin and the others edged closer towards us, looking curious. 'He wants to have a word.'

'How are you, Georgie?' Ray Hilton smiled down at me from what seemed to be a very great height – he was ginormous! 'Nice to meet you. I just wanted to tell you that you've got the makings of a very good goalie. I know it's not easy to make a career out of football, for girls or boys, but you're on the right track. Keep learning, keep practising and you'll get even better than you already are.'

'Thanks,' I managed to stammer at last.

'And make sure you listen to Ria,' Ray advised, a twinkle in his eyes. 'She knows what she's talking about!'

I nodded, glancing a little warily at Ria who smiled at me. Ray Hilton chatted to me for a few more minutes, asking how long I'd been playing and so on, and I got him to autograph my Open Day programme. Then he and Ria went off together. Instantly the other girls surrounded me, slapping me on the back.

'Way to go, Georgie!' Hannah exclaimed, giving me a squeeze.

'Did you hear that, you two?' Jasmin called to Luke and Jack who'd also been listening to my conversation with Ray Hilton, but were pretending they weren't. 'Ray Hilton thinks Georgie's ace.'

'Well, he *was* wearing glasses!' Luke teased. But he winked at me, and I knew he was pleased.

And as for me – well, I was thrilled! When I thought about how miserable I'd been for the last few weeks, this was my best day in a long, long time. It wasn't perfect, I thought, as I noticed Dad smiling at Ria as he handed her a can of lemonade. There were still things that *might* happen that I didn't want to think about. But there was plenty of footie to be played, the Stars were on track for promotion, I was getting along better with Luke and Jack and I had all my mates around me. Life was GOOD.

'Let's celebrate the new, improved Georgie Taylor with a milkshake!' I suggested.

And that's exactly what we did.

THE BEAUTIFUL GAME

WIN £50 TOPSHOP VOUCHERS!

Just answer the following questions:

1. What is the name of Georgie's cat?
2. Which country does Freya move to?
3. What is the name of the footballer Georgie meets at the Open Day?

Log on to

www.thebeautifulgamebooks.co.uk

NOW for your chance to win!

Or send a postcard with your answers and your name and address to: The Beautiful Game Competition, Orchard Marketing Department, 338 Euston Road, London NW1 3BH.

Full terms and conditions are available online.
Competition closes 30th June 2010.

THE
BEAUTIFUL
GAME

Look out for the next book in
The Beautiful Game series!

978 1 40830 424 2 £5.99

Coming soon!

About the Author

Narinder Dhami lives in Cambridge with her husband Robert and their three cats, but was originally born in Wolverhampton. Her dad came over from India in 1954, and met and married her mum, who is English. Narinder always wanted to write, but after university taught in London for ten years before becoming a writer.

For the last thirteen years Narinder has been a full-time author. She has written over 100 children's books, as well as many short stories and articles for children's magazines. *Georgie's War* is the third book in The Beautiful Game series.

Since her childhood, Narinder has been a huge football fan.

A message from the England Women's Captain
FAYE WHITE

With over 1.5 million playing the game, girls' and women's football is now the number one female sport. I have played for Arsenal and England ladies since I was sixteen. I grew up kicking a ball around – in the playground, at school, or in my back garden. I was the only girl playing amongst boys, but I never let that stop me, and I joined my first club at thirteen.

For me, playing football has always been about passion and enjoyment. It's a great way to challenge myself, be active, gain self-confidence, and learn about teamwork.

I have gone on to captain and play for England seventy times, and achieved my dream of playing in a World Cup (China 2007). I've won over twenty-five honours for Arsenal, including the treble, and the Women's UEFA Cup.

Do you love football as much as me?
Then maybe, just maybe, you can follow in my shoes...
Practice, be passionate and strive for your dream. Enjoy!

Find out more about Faye and girls' football at...

www.faye-white.co.uk   www.thefa.com/womens
www.arsenal.com/ladies   www.fairgamemagazine.co.uk